"Did he hurt you?" Jake asked.

"No." Tara's reply, muffled yet strong, kept him from turning the truck around and killing the man.

"What happened to your leg?"

"Nothing."

"Honey, you limped all the way to my truck."

"I know," she said and then she started to cry in earnest. Jake tightened his hold around Tara. With the tip of his finger, he tilted her chin up and looked at her face. Her small brown freckles looked stark against the paleness of her skin. Her eyes and nose were red and tear streaks stained her cheeks. Wisps of her strawberry-blond hair, wet with tears, clung to her face.

He took his free hand and tucked her hair behind her ears. With the pad of his thumb, he traced the tear streaks.

Tara sighed, her sweet pink lips parting just slightly.

He bent down.

She lifted her chin just enough.

Jake kissed her. And when she wrapped both arms around his neck, pulling him closer, pushing her breasts up against his chest, he thought he might never stop kissing her….

BEVERLY LONG

RUNNING FOR HER LIFE

For Jim—a wonderful brother-in-law and a dear friend. You were an inspiration to me and to everyone else who had the privilege of knowing you.

Recycling programs for this product may not exist in your area.

ISBN-13: 978-0-373-74709-2

RUNNING FOR HER LIFE

This edition published by arrangement with Harlequin Books S.A.

For questions and comments about the quality of this book, please contact us at CustomerService@Harlequin.com.

www.Harlequin.com

Printed in U.S.A.

ABOUT THE AUTHOR

As a child, Beverly Long used to take a flashlight to bed so that she could hide under the covers and read. Once a teenager, more often than not, the books she chose were romance novels. Now she gets to keep the light on as long as she wants, and there's always a romance novel on her nightstand. With both a bachelor's and a master's degree in business and more than twenty years of experience as a human resources director, she now enjoys the opportunity to write her own stories. She considers her books to be a great success if they compel the reader to stay up way past his or her bedtime.

Beverly loves to hear from readers. Visit www.beverlylong.com or like her at www.facebook.com/BeverlyLong.Romance.

Books by Beverly Long

HARLEQUIN INTRIGUE

1388—RUNNING FOR HER LIFE

CAST OF CHARACTERS

Tara Thompson—She loves her café and the people in Wyattville, Minnesota, but believes she may have to run again to stay one step ahead of her abusive ex-fiancé.

Chief Jake Vernelli—He's a big-city cop with temporary duty in a small town. He's certain that Tara is hiding something. Will he figure out her secret in time or will he once again lose someone important?

Michael Watson Masterly—He'd almost killed Tara once. Has he tracked her down in Wyattville and is he biding his time before he strikes the final blow?

Alice Fenton—She is Tara's friend and landlord, but she harbors resentment toward Tara for something her son told her.

Donny Miso—An angry, out-of-work man who has lost just about everything. Is he desperate enough to hurt Tara, the one person who has treated him well?

Jim Waller—He holds a prestigious position at the bank, but suddenly he has an unexpected interest in Tara that puts her in danger.

Madeline Fenton—Her past is filled with secrets and she could destroy everything that Tara has worked for. Or is it her brother, Bill, who is the dangerous one?

Bill Fenton—He's left Wyattville and is supposedly moving on. Is it possible that he's angry because Tara wanted only to be friends?

Chapter One

Jake Vernelli flicked his windshield wipers to high and tightened his grip on the steering wheel of his 1969 GMC pickup. On a pleasant summer night, there'd be another hour of daylight but there wasn't anything pleasant about this night. It was dark and ugly and it matched Jake's mood perfectly.

When Chase had described Wyattville, Minnesota, his old friend had been characteristically kind. *It's a little remote.*

Remote? Hell, all signs of civilization had faded away when Jake had left the interstate for a bumpy, narrow, two-lane road. More than once, he'd considered making one big U-turn and pointing the nose of his truck back toward Minneapolis. But Chase's telephone call from last week was fresh enough that he could still hear the desperation in the man's voice.

Please, Jake. It's only for six weeks. I wouldn't ask if I had any other options.

And that was fact. In all the years they'd known

each other, Chase had never once asked and had offered more times than Jake could count. The most recent offer had come two months ago, just days after Jake had tried to turn in his badge.

He'd told Chase he was fine, that the gunshot wound was healing nicely, and that he'd put Marcy's funeral behind him. It was the first time he'd ever lied to his friend. But what was he supposed to say? That he thought about his dead partner every single day and wondered just how he'd missed that she was in trouble?

Could he admit that he'd thought about how miserably lucky he'd been that he'd only gotten a bullet in his leg while young Officer Howard, who'd had the bad luck to get caught in the crossfire between him and Marcy, had lost his life? Should he disclose that in the middle of the night, when his soul felt most tortured, that he questioned whether it had been for naught? Marcy had died but there would still be drugs on the street, in the schoolyard, everywhere. Should he confess that he wasn't sure he could make a big enough difference anymore?

It was better to lie.

And pretend that he was moving on.

Jake stretched and grabbed the flashlight that had slipped into the crack between the bench seat and the passenger-side door. He pointed it at the directions he'd received just that afternoon. Once satisfied that his navigation was sound, he flicked the light off and glanced ahead.

Fifty feet in front of him, a deer stood in the middle of the damn road.

He flattened the palm of his hand on the horn, pressed his foot hard on the brake, and felt his heart jump when the back tires of his truck lost traction on the wet road.

The bed of the truck slammed into the guardrail, and suddenly he was rolling. His seat belt jerked tight and something, maybe the flashlight, struck him a glancing blow on his chin. The truck rolled a second time and then stopped so suddenly that Jake cracked the left side of his forehead on something.

"Damn it." He fumbled for the interior light, switched it on and took stock. The cab looked fine, and he felt ridiculously pleased that Veronica was built like a tank. The only problem was, she had metal trim around the doors, and he was pretty sure that was what he'd cracked his head against. He flipped down his visor and looked into the small mirror. The area above his left eye was already swelling, and in the dim interior light he could see fresh blood oozing from a thin cut.

He peered out the windshield. His headlights were still on, but all he could see through the driving rain was two-feet-high grass. Everywhere. He'd landed in some kind of gulley. His truck was in

Drive and the engine was running, but he wasn't going anywhere.

He pulled his cell phone out of his shirt pocket, turned it on and waited. It beeped twice and then the screen went dark. He shook it, turned it on again and met with similar results.

The hinterlands evidently didn't get cell phone service.

He shoved the truck into Park, pulled the key and unbuckled his seat belt. Using his flashlight, he saw that there was solid earth reaching halfway up the door. He scooted across the seat and looked. Same damn thing.

He opened his glove compartment, retrieved his gun and stuck it into the waistband of his pants. Then he pulled his dark green rain poncho out from underneath the seat, shook out the wrinkles with one sharp flick of his wrist and slipped the thin plastic over his head. Finally, using the butt of the flashlight as a battering ram, he knocked out a perfectly good windshield and crawled out.

Once he stood on Veronica's hood, he realized that it was a mere foot aboveground. It was going to take a tow truck and somebody who knew what they were doing to get him out of there. The wind took his breath away and the rain beat at him as thunder rumbled and lightning streaked across the dark sky. It was a horrible night to be out, but waiting for someone to pass by wasn't much of a plan. He hadn't seen another car for the past half hour.

Before long some animal would probably mosey by and eat him. He pulled up his hood and started walking.

TARA THOMPSON PARKED her twelve-year-old van in the dark garage, thankful that she'd managed to keep the beast on the slick roads. It had been raining hard when she'd left the café and harder still just seconds ago, when she'd jumped out to open the garage door. Shivering in her wet clothes, she pulled down the heavy wood door and stood underneath the small overhang the roof offered. She could barely see her farmhouse, just thirty feet away.

Taking a deep breath, she sprinted. She took the two steps in one leap, yanked open the screen door, unlocked the interior door and threw herself inside. Heart racing, feeling almost giddy, she leaned against her back door and tried to catch her breath.

She could hear the rain pound against the new shingles that her landlord had laboriously laid just weeks earlier. When she flipped the light switch next to the door and saw that the only thing dripping on the kitchen floor was her, she smiled. Maybe Henry had been right when he promised that her bucket days were over.

She kicked off her wet shoes just as a bolt of

lightning hit close enough to shake her house. The lights went out without so much as a flicker. She stood in the dark, waiting, hoping. Minutes ticked off and giddiness seeped away, replaced by grim determination.

Reaching into the cupboard above the stove, she grabbed a candle, then matches. It took just seconds to locate the tall glass she'd left drying upside down next to the sink. She righted it, stuck a candle in it and on her second try got the match to spark.

She held the glass above her head and peered into the cupboard. She found four more candles and pulled them all out, hoping they would be enough. In the fourteen months she'd been living in eastern Minnesota, the electricity had gone out at least three times. Six months ago, during a February ice storm, it had been off for almost forty-eight hours.

Hot shower came off the to-do list. No electricity meant no power to the pump on the well, which meant no running water. The best she could do was peel off the clothes she'd been wearing for the past twelve hours. She picked up the glass, and as she walked up the narrow stairway to the second floor, the slim candle swayed from side to side, bouncing light off the pale walls.

In her bedroom, she undressed. Even her bra and panties were wet. She scooped up her clothes and tossed them into the hamper, feeling the pull in her shoulders. It had been three days since Donny had up and quit. She needed to get a new dishwasher hired. The extra work was taking its toll.

In the mirror, she saw the shadow of unpaid invoices and half-completed order forms on the corner of her old desk. She'd planned on catching up earlier in the week and had told herself on the way home that tonight was it. No lights meant no guilt about putting the nagging paperwork aside. She smiled, blew out the candle and flopped down on the bed.

The wind was even stronger now and the lightning and thunder almost simultaneous, telling her that the full brunt of the storm had hit. The rain had turned to hail and it crashed against the windows as if someone was throwing buckets of marbles against the small house.

It was a cacophony of noise—wild and bold and oddly rhythmic. She closed her eyes, content to think of nothing, content to let the strain of the busy day slip away. However, minutes later, more asleep than awake, a pounding on her back door had her jerking up in bed.

Nobody ever came to her back door.

That is, nobody except Henry. She took a breath and felt the tightness in her chest ease up. Her landlord had stopped by the restaurant shortly after the noon rush and promised that he'd be over later to fix the loose tile on her bathroom floor. That was before the sky had unzipped and rained on her parade.

He should not be out on a night like this. She scrambled off the bed and slipped on the pale blue cotton robe that hung on the back of her bedroom door. On the way out, she grabbed the glass and unlit candle off her dresser.

Good Lord. She loved the old fool like the father she'd lost, but this was ridiculous. He'd be soaked. Probably get pneumonia and she'd never hear the end of it. "If you don't stop beating the heck out of my screen door, you'll be fixing that, too," she mumbled. The stairway was pitch-black; she grabbed the railing with her free hand and stepped carefully.

Once downstairs, she stopped just long enough to light the candle and set it on the coffee table. "Hang on," she yelled. She realized he hadn't heard her over the storm when the pounding continued. She went to the door and pulled back the curtain on the window. He was hunched over, wearing his ratty rain poncho. She fumbled with the lock and finally whipped open the door. Wind and rain blew in.

"Are you crazy?" she yelled, yanking on Henry's sleeve. She pulled him into the house. At least the man had enough sense to put his hood up. "Alice is going to skin you alive," she said.

"Who's Alice?"

Tara jumped back, knocking into the hall table. And in the next second, when he turned and the light from the candle on the coffee table caught his profile, she knew exactly who was crazy.

She was.

She'd let a stranger into her house. He was big and broad-shouldered, and from what she could see of his face, he wasn't happy. Then he pushed his hood back and she saw bloody raw skin on his forehead.

She screamed and ran. He managed to catch her before she got through the front door. She had it open just inches when he reached over her shoulder and slammed it shut with the palm of his hand. Whirling around, she thrust an elbow toward his face.

"Calm down," he said.

She would not give in—not this time. She shoved and kicked but it was like hitting a damn wall.

"Stop it," he said, using both hands to grab her flailing arms. With one hand, he pinned her arms over her head. With his other free hand, he grasped her chin. "You're going to hurt yourself," he warned.

She didn't want to beg. But fear robbed her voice of strength. "Let go of me," she whispered.

When he didn't, she brought her knee up. He managed to twist out of the way. Then he wrapped an arm around her middle, picked her up so that her feet were kicking wildly in the air, carried her five feet over to the couch and dumped her on it.

She expected him to fall on top of her, but instead he backed up a couple steps, practically tripping over the coffee table in his haste to get away. Scooting to the corner of the couch, she pulled her old robe tight. She felt naked and vulnerable, and she thought she might throw up.

Why hadn't she been more careful? She'd been so cautious for fourteen months and now, in one instant, it was all for nothing.

Never taking his eyes off her, he moved sideways, far enough that he could flip the switch on the wall. When nothing happened, he looked at the candle and she saw bleak acceptance in his eyes. He pulled a flashlight out of his pocket, turned it on and swept the space that served as a combined kitchen and family room. His gaze rested on the sink and she knew he saw the lone clean plate and coffee cup.

It didn't matter. She wasn't going to make it easy for him. The minute he came closer, she was going to grab the lamp and hit him with it. She was going to use her fingernails, her teeth, anything she could.

But when he moved, it wasn't forward. He sank down on the love seat. "I'm sorry," he said. "I didn't mean to scare you. I looked in the garage window and saw a van. I thought somebody might be home."

"Get out of my house," she said, her voice low.

"I was in an accident." He pointed to his forehead. "My truck is in a ditch, a deep one, about a mile from here. I'm not sure how badly it's damaged. My cell didn't work. All I want is to use your telephone to call a garage so that I can get the son of a—" he hesitated "—gun out of there."

Could he be telling the truth? She held her arm to her side, the rough, scarred skin pressing against her ribs, separated only by the thin robe. Rain always made the bone ache. Getting pushed up against the front door hadn't helped.

She'd run on instinct. She'd fought when cornered.

That brought her some comfort. As hard as she'd fought, however, she knew the stranger was big enough and strong enough that he could have easily hurt her. But instead, he'd backed off and was giving her a chance to calm down. Was it some kind of trick?

Or was it possible that he hadn't come looking for her, that Michael hadn't sent him? That he'd simply crashed his vehicle, knocked his head in the process, and her house had been the first he'd stumbled upon? "Where was the accident?"

"A mile or so south. I'm on my way to Wyattville," he continued. "Please tell me that I'm headed in the right direction."

She wasn't telling him anything. Not until she knew why he was here. "What's your name?" she demanded.

"Jake Vernelli." He reached into his jeans pocket and pulled out a wallet. From his poncho pocket, he pulled out what appeared to be a hastily folded sheet of paper. After flipping open the wallet, he tried to smooth out the crumpled paper.

She leaned forward. The picture on the license was of him, sans bloody forehead. With a practiced eye for taking in details quickly, she scanned it. Dark hair, olive skin, classic Italian appearance. Six-two, 190 pounds. He'd be thirty-three in two weeks, making him almost exactly a year older than her. The name on it was Jake Vernelli.

She shifted her gaze to the paper. It was a fax sent from the law offices of Chase Montgomery. Chase had been elected mayor the previous year and when she scanned the fax, she remembered the gossip she'd heard at the restaurant just that morning. The mayor had called a childhood friend and arranged for him to fill in for Chief Wilks, who'd had a heart attack and then bypass surgery.

"Do you know Chief Wilks?" he asked.

She nodded. She liked the chief; everybody did. But she'd never really felt comfortable around him.

Michael had gotten to the police once before, he could do it again.

"I'm taking his place for six weeks," he said.

Tara's stomach tightened. "So you're a cop?"

"That's right." He swallowed deliberately. "Given the circumstances, I would think you might consider that a positive."

Hardly. She was living way outside the law.

Chapter Two

"You broke into my house," she accused.

"I did not break in." He said it so fast his words were clipped. "You opened the door and *pulled* me in."

His head injury couldn't be too serious. "I suppose I did."

"What's your name?" he asked.

She didn't want to tell him. There was something about this man, something about the intensity of his gaze, the edginess of his attitude. Would he see things that others had simply looked past? Would he find a loose thread and pull at it until her life unraveled?

"Tara Thompson," she said, as if she'd been saying it her whole life. She got up, walked ten feet to her kitchen counter, pulled out a drawer and felt around for the small box of plastic bags. Then she opened the freezer door and filled the bag with ice. She gently tossed it in his direction. "You've got a pretty good-sized bump."

"Thanks," he said. He held the ice bag up to his forehead. "Who's Alice?" he repeated his very first question.

"Alice Fenton. She and her husband, Henry, are my landlords. They live one crossroad over." She wiped the palm of her hand on her old robe. "Do you think you need to see a doctor?"

"So that I can hear that I'm going to have a hell of a headache for a couple of days?" He smiled and it was such a startling change to his serious demeanor that she was thrown off balance.

She stepped back and rammed her spine against the kitchen counter. He studied her. And while there wasn't enough light at this distance to clearly see his eyes, the tilt of his head, the subtle thrust of his chin, told her that he was assessing, considering. Wondering.

It was the look of a man who might be interested, maybe even intrigued, by a woman. It made her feel warm and vulnerable in a whole different way and she yanked on the belt of her robe, pulling it tighter. The worn material rubbed against her nipples and she was grateful for the darkness, grateful that he couldn't see that his look affected her.

She jerked open the kitchen drawer and pulled out a bottle of hydrogen peroxide. She grabbed a tissue box and carried both back to the coffee table. She placed them next to the burning candle. "You should probably clean that scrape. There's no water but this will be better anyway."

She moved back to her spot in the kitchen. He grabbed a few tissues and tipped the brown bottle to its side. After taking a couple swipes across his forehead, he got up and tossed the bloody tissue into the waste can at the end of her kitchen counter. Her stomach jumped in response. She hated blood. Could never quite forget the sight of it running down her arm, dripping onto the floor.

"Thank you," he said.

"Sure," she managed. *Think about something else.* It was generally good advice. However, when he rubbed his hand over his jaw and, like a crazy woman, she felt the answering response low in her belly—as if he'd rubbed the palm of his hand intimately against her—she realized it was a mistake. He was a stranger. A cop. She had no business thinking about warmth against warmth, about callused skin against absolute softness. About what it might be like to be held again.

"About my truck?" he asked.

She swallowed hard. "Of course. Toby Wilson owns the local garage. He sells gas and does some basic body work. Some nights he works late so you might get lucky." She reached to dial the telephone just as it rang.

"Hello," she said tentatively. She rarely got calls.

"Tara, this is Frank Johnson. There's been some trouble in town."

She gripped the receiver more tightly. "What kind of trouble?"

"Looks as if somebody damaged your front door, broke out the glass, anyway. It doesn't look as if they got in but I'm not sure."

She couldn't breathe. Couldn't think. She'd been in Wyattville all this time and nothing had happened. Why now?

"Tara?" Frank prompted.

"I'll be there as soon as I can." Tara hung up and whirled around, almost bumping into the new chief.

"What's wrong?" he demanded.

"I own a restaurant in town. There's been some damage."

"From the storm?"

"No. At least that's what Frank Johnson said. He owns the drugstore next door." She tried to speak slowly, calmly, but it was impossible. Fourteen months ago, in a rage, Michael had shredded dresses and slashed artwork. Had he found a new way to torment her by vandalizing her business?

She didn't want to have to run again.

"Tara?"

She stared at him.

"You looked as if you were a million miles away."

Thirteen hundred miles. But was it far enough? "I have to go." She glanced around the dark kitchen.

Where had she dropped her purse? It didn't matter. She grabbed her keys off the counter and took a step toward the door.

"You might want to get dressed first," he suggested.

Of course. What she needed to do was stop freaking out. If Michael had found her, she'd need her wits about her. And she needed to get rid of Jake Vernelli. "I can drop you off in town," she said.

He shrugged. "I think I've gathered enough to know that my first day on the job just started early."

"But what about your truck?"

"Trust me on this. It's not going anywhere."

She wasn't going to be able to shake him. But she couldn't worry about that now. She lit another candle, kept her keys gripped in her hand while she found another glass and then used it to light the way up the stairs where she pulled on underwear, jeans and a long-sleeved white shirt. When she came back to the living room, he was standing by her back door. She slipped her feet into the still-wet sandals that she'd shed earlier. When she reached for the door, he put his hand on her arm. Heat shot upward, settling somewhere around her collarbone.

"Are you okay to drive?" he asked.

"Yes."

He didn't argue. Instead, he blew out both candles. Then they ran through the rain, dodging puddles. He opened the garage door before she had a chance to. "Pull out and I'll close it behind us," he said.

SHE DROVE FAST and they arrived in the small town just minutes later. A police cruiser, its lights flashing, sat crossways in the middle of the street, keeping cars from getting past. The streetlights were on, and lights shined through windows up and down the street, telling Jake that the power outage hadn't included Wyattville.

Tara jerked the wheel to the right, pulled into a parking spot and bolted from her car. A man pushing sixty, standing in front of the drugstore, saw her and waved. She took four steps before Jake caught up with her.

"Stay behind me," he said, stepping in front of her.

Jake could see the momentary indecision and thought he might just have to tackle her. Given the curves he'd glimpsed under her thin blue robe, the very same ones that were hugged tight by her white shirt and jeans, it wouldn't be much of a sacrifice. Knowing his luck, though, she'd bring her damn knee up again and hit pay dirt and he'd start his job walking funny for days.

"Fine," she said through clenched teeth.

He moved quickly, Tara on his heels. Fortunately most of the businesses had awnings, so they could stay out of the rain as they ran toward the man standing on the sidewalk.

"Mr. Johnson?" Jake asked.

"Yes. Who are you?"

"I'm Jake Vernelli."

The older man smiled. "The new guy. I'm on the city council and let me tell you, we're damn glad you were available. I don't want you to get the wrong idea here. Generally, Wyattville is a pretty quiet place."

Tara stepped out from behind him. "What happened, Frank?"

"Officer Hooper drove by around nine and everything was fine, but when he cruised through at ten, he saw that the front door of Nel's looked odd. I was at the store late and saw him outside. I called you right away."

Jake could tell by the slump of Tara's shoulders that everything definitely wasn't okay. He adjusted his angle slightly. Nel's Café had a big door that was wood on the bottom and frosted glass on the top. Two inches above where the wood stopped and the glass began was a round hole. Bigger than a golf ball, maybe the right size for a baseball. Around it, the glass had splintered in a semicircle, with cracks shooting upward. It looked similar to how a first grader might draw the sun on a pretty summer day.

Jake walked closer, leaned down and attempted to peer through the hole. It was dark inside. There were two large windows on either side of the door. Unfortunately, the blinds were down, completely eliminating any assistance the streetlights might have given.

"Crazy night for somebody to be out causing trouble," Frank said. "Probably just some kids without anything better to do."

"Oh, sure," she said. And Jake wouldn't have thought much about it if she hadn't followed up the comment with a quick but deliberate look over her right shoulder, then her left. It was her eyes that pulled at Jake's gut. She had the look of someone waiting for the other shoe to drop.

A young officer dressed in a khaki uniform approached. His brown buzzed hair looked official, but the flushed face and sweat stains under his arms didn't inspire confidence. *Green.* That was how Chase had described Andy Hooper. He covered the evening shift and would share call with Jake for the night shift.

Frank Johnson stepped forward. "Andy, this here is your new boss, Jake Vernelli."

Andy stuck out his hand. "Pleasure to meet you. Mayor Montgomery said good things about you, sir."

Chase must have left out the part about shooting his partner. Jake returned the shake. "Good to meet you," he said. "What happened here tonight?"

The young officer flipped open his notebook.

"Front door is damaged. Back door appears untouched. There are no witnesses. It does not appear that entry was gained. I was waiting for Tara to get here with a key so I could check out the inside."

The kid had needed to consult his notes for that? It was going to be a long six weeks.

With her keys in hand, Tara started toward the door. Jake knew it was unlikely there was any danger. An intruder would have needed to manage getting his or her arm through the hole, enough to flip the lock from inside. That would have been difficult to do with without causing more glass to break. However, he'd seen a lot of odd things in his career.

Jake held out his hands for her keys. "Not until Officer Hooper and I check it out," he said. He pulled his gun from the waistband of his jeans and he saw the immediate question in Frank Johnson's eyes: *Is that really necessary?*

Hell, he had no idea. But it hadn't been that long ago that he'd been almost too slow to pull his gun, and he didn't intend to make that mistake again. When Officer Hooper hurried to get his own weapon, Jake fought the instinct to duck and run.

Jake unlocked the door and kicked it open with his foot, wide enough that they could enter. With the door open, there was enough light that he could quickly scan the dim interior. There were tables on one side, booths on the other. An aisle down the middle led to a long counter with six stools. Behind the counter were the pop machine, milk machine and stacks of glasses. "I'm going to check the kitchen," he whispered. "Stay here."

He walked toward the swinging door at the rear of the restaurant. However, instead of opening it, he veered behind the counter and walked toward the service window that was cut into the rear wall. It was chest high, three feet long by eighteen inches high, perfect for getting the hot food from the stove to the table in an express manner. He peered through the opening.

Toward the back, a light burning over a three-compartment sink made it possible to see the grill, stove and steam table on one side, refrigerator and worktable on the other. Across from the sink, behind a half wall, was the dishwasher. Beyond it, a rear entrance that looked undisturbed.

"It's clear. Tell Tara that she can come in."

By the time he got to the front of the restaurant, she was standing next to the cash register. The drawer was open and the slots were empty. "You keep any money in here?" he asked.

Tara shook her head. "After we close up in the afternoon, I make a deposit at the bank. I hold back enough to start the drawer out in the morning but I keep it in the kitchen."

"Freezer, right?"

She smiled and it reached her eyes—her very pretty moss-green eyes. They went nicely with her hair—a rich, more strawberry than blond mix that touched her shoulders.

"Too obvious," she said. "I use a mixing bowl."

"Go check it and make sure it's all there," he said.

He flipped on a light and looked around. The place wasn't fancy but it looked spotless, and the combination of colors—blues, greens and browns—made it welcoming. He picked up a menu, scanned it and almost laughed at how reasonable the prices were. Okay, there was one good thing about small towns.

It took him about fifteen seconds to find the baseball lodged underneath one of the wooden booths. "Andy, you got an evidence bag in your car?" he asked.

"Yes, sir."

"Chief Vernelli is fine. Go get it."

The kid was back so fast with a bag, gloves and a camera that Jake was pretty sure he'd run. Had he ever been that eager to please? God knew he'd loved being a cop. Had never contemplated that he'd walk away from it.

He snapped a few photos before putting on the gloves and carefully picking up the ball. He'd just put it in the bag when Tara returned. "We'll dust it for prints but if it was kids, they likely won't have a record," Jake said.

"This is the kind of stuff kids do, right?"

She sounded almost hopeful. The last teenager he'd arrested had stolen a car. The one before that had stabbed his mother. "Anybody in particular who might be pissed off at you? Fired any high school help lately?"

She shook her head. "No. I did have a dishwasher leave, but I didn't fire him—he quit. And he wasn't a kid. Probably in his early thirties."

"Why did he quit?"

"I don't know. I would have appreciated some notice but he just left a message on my voice mail that he wouldn't be back. I hope he found a better job. He took this after he lost his position when his company outsourced their manufacturing to China."

Dishwasher. He hadn't contemplated that as a career choice when he'd been up at two in the morning, wondering just what the hell he was going to do if he couldn't be a cop anymore. He could go from scraping garbage off the street to scraping food off plates. "Name?"

"Donny Miso."

Easy enough to remember. Jake walked to the front door and snapped a couple more photos. He handed the camera back to Andy. "I'll finish up here," he told the young officer. "I think you can probably move the squad out of the street now," he added.

Jake watched Officer Hooper lope down the sidewalk. When he was almost at his car, Jake turned toward Tara. "Something tells me that he doesn't get to use the lights and siren very often."

She smiled. "He means well." She squatted and grabbed a piece of glass and promptly sliced open the tip of her index finger. Blood welled up from the cut. He moved to her side and grabbed her wrist to get a closer look.

"Go wash that out," he said. "I'll take care of this."

"That's not necessary," she protested weakly. She was looking at the blood on her finger. Her face had lost its natural color, making the freckles on her nose stand out.

She started walking back to the kitchen. He followed.

"What are you doing?" she asked, looking over her shoulder.

"Making sure you don't fall over," he said, deciding truth was the best option. He'd noticed her reaction to the bloody wipe earlier and had better understood why she'd freaked when he'd pulled back his hood and she'd suddenly been up close and personal with the blood streaking down his face. Everybody had their Achilles' heel.

She squared her shoulders. "I am *not* going to fall down."

Soft curves and a rod of steel up her backbone. Hell of a combination. "Okay." He turned back toward the dining room. He picked up the larger pieces of glass, all the while listening for unusual sounds in the kitchen. He was almost done when there was a shadow in the doorway. He looked up and saw Frank.

"I got a piece of plywood to nail over the window," he said.

"Perfect." Jake walked outside and it took only a couple minutes for the two men to nail the covering in place.

Frank shook his hand when they were finished. "Welcome, Jake. By the way, my daughter Lori Mae is your daytime dispatcher and department secretary. If you want to know anything, she can tell you. And if I can be of assistance, let me know. In fact, if you've got the time tomorrow, we could meet for a cup of coffee here at Nel's, say ten?"

"I'll see you then," Jake said. When he stepped inside the restaurant, Tara was standing near the door.

"You've been busy," she said, motioning to the floor and the window.

"Frank helped. Seems like a nice guy."

She nodded. "When I opened the restaurant fourteen months ago, he was my first customer, and he's eaten lunch here every day since then."

"Did you grow up in Wyattville?"

She shook her head. "I moved here from Florida."

He'd spent five of the worst weeks of his life in

Miami, working undercover, sniffing out drug dealers. "Where at in Florida?"

It might have been his imagination but he thought she pulled back a little. "We moved around a lot," she said. "You know, I'm really tired. I should finish up here so that I can get home at a reasonable hour."

She didn't need to hit him over the head with a baseball bat. And it wasn't as if he really wanted her life story. No matter how cute she was, he was a short-timer, and in six weeks he'd have paid his debt back to his friend. Then he was driving back to Minneapolis and forgetting about this wide spot in the road.

"I still need to get in contact with Toby Wilson about Veronica. My truck," he added quickly.

She didn't bat an eye that he'd named his truck. Just grabbed the pen that was next to the cash register, tore a napkin out of the two-sided dispenser on the counter and scribbled a number down. "There's a phone in the kitchen."

For a second time, he yanked the directions to Chase Montgomery's house out of his pocket. "By my calculations, Chase's house should be just a couple blocks from here. I'll call from there."

"I heard he was out of town, visiting his parents. Something about his mother being ill."

"That's right. He'll be back in a couple weeks. I'm going to stay at his house while I'm covering for Chief Wilks." He walked toward the door. "By the way," he added, "watch out for the deer when you're driving home."

Once again her eyes flicked toward the street. He got the strangest feeling that whatever or whoever it was that Tara Thompson was watching out for, it didn't have four legs.

Chapter Three

It was still dark when Tara woke up. The light was blinking on her alarm clock, telling her that sometime during the night the electricity had come back on. She reached for the switch on the lamp and glanced at her watch. Ten minutes before five. In one smooth movement, she stretched and rolled out of bed. She pulled on a running bra, shorts and a shirt, and sat on the edge of the mattress while she laced up her shoes. After a quick stop in the bathroom, she bounced down the steps, grabbed a bottle of water on her way past the refrigerator and was out the door. The sun had not yet crested the horizon but night had faded, leaving the quiet countryside bathed in a soft blue-gray.

She jogged for the first quarter of a mile, then picked up the pace. With each step, she felt stronger, sturdier, more confident. She hadn't been a runner when she'd lived in D.C. She'd rarely exercised, choosing to spend what little free time she had with Michael. But shortly after settling in Wyattville, she'd started jogging and lifting weights. She hadn't been worried about her jeans zipping. She'd simply been focused on getting strong.

If Michael ever got lucky enough to find her, she needed to be both physically and mentally ready. The head stuff was harder. But she was making progress. It had been months since she'd had one of the nightmares that had plagued her when she'd first come to Wyattville. She knew she'd turned the corner when she'd dreamed that he'd found her and she—dressed like Catwoman, but hey, it was a dream—had kicked his butt.

She tried to get in three miles several times a week, generally before work. If she kept her pace steady, she could get to Wyattville, turn around and be home in time to jump in the shower and still make it to work with ten minutes to spare.

Normally when she ran, her mind emptied out. There was no room to worry about leaky water pipes or a temperamental fryer that had a touchy on-off switch. She was consumed with the cadence of her steps, the harshness of her breath, the pure thrill of pushing herself to the limit. Absolute freedom from thought. It was all good.

But not today. She was tired and edgy and felt stupid because she'd lost sleep over a broken window. It wasn't as if she'd been robbed at gunpoint. She was getting soft. There'd been a time when crime was part of her everyday life. She'd talked about it, wondered about it and even joked about it. Most every reporter at the paper had.

Not that many would have admitted to the last. After all, everyone knew it wasn't a joke. But in a city where even murder seemed routine, laughter was the coping mechanism of choice.

That was life B.W. Before Wyattville. Now she talked about the weather, wondered about the price of lettuce and laughed at dumb jokes that her customers told her. It still hardly seemed possible. Nel's Main Street Café had gone on the market the week before Tara had come through Wyattville on her way to nowhere. She took one look at the cozy little diner and paid cash for it two days later. It had eaten up every bit of her savings. But somehow she'd known it was the right thing to do.

And every day for the past fourteen months, she'd been thankful. She'd had a reason to get up, to get dressed, to work hard. A reason to forget.

Although some memories were harder to shake than others. She extended her arms straight from her shoulders, automatically noting the slight difference in the length. Her arms were covered, like always. No matter how sweaty she got running or how steamy the kitchen became, she didn't dare let people see the damage. There'd be too many questions, too much speculation. She didn't need the constant reminder, either. Didn't need to look at the two scars on her right arm that ran seven inches long and a sixteenth of an inch wide, crossing over each other at the bend in her elbow, to remember the pain, the absolute terror. The orthopedic surgeons had told her the pink, slightly puckered skin would continue to fade until it turned completely white some day.

She supposed that was true. Her arm looked better than it had fourteen months ago, although it was still hideous. And as crazy as it sounded, she was almost grateful for it. The injury had made her realize that ultimately Michael would kill her. It was the push she'd needed to leave her fiancé behind, to leave her life behind.

Otherwise, she'd have been one of the crime stories they reported in the early edition. Maybe one of the ones they laughed about, or shook their heads about.

She'd made a life here in Wyattville. It was a different life than the one she'd left behind, but still, a good life. And most important, she'd felt safe here.

And she still did. She wasn't going to let a busted window change that.

The summer air was already thick with humidity, and sweat trickled down her front and back. There was barely a breeze on her bare legs. She sipped on her water bottle and pushed herself harder.

She was less than a mile from town when she saw a car crest the hill. Without breaking stride, she edged farther to the side of the road, onto the hard-packed gravel that bordered the blacktop. She'd just lifted her hand in a neighborly wave when the car swerved, gunning straight for her.

JAKE DESPERATELY NEEDED COFFEE. On his best days, he didn't generally participate in any real conversation until he'd had his first cup followed by two or three quick refills. And he wasn't at his best today. He hadn't slept well. Wanted to believe it was because he'd been in a strange bed in a strange house with six weeks of duty facing him. But he suspected it had less to do with that and more to do with a strawberry-blonde with freckles on her nose and pretty green eyes.

Chase had left a brief note, wishing him well, along with keys to a cruiser that matched the car Andy Hooper had been driving the previous night. There were also a couple sets of uniforms. After waking up, he'd showered, pulled on a pair of khaki pants, a shirt that fit well enough, and buckled the standard-issue duty belt that Chase had left hanging over the door.

Now, fifteen minutes after his feet had hit the floor, he was in the car, headed toward Nel's Café. The night before, he'd seen the sign on the door, indicating that business hours started at six and ended at three. He parked, got out, and could see that someone had turned the blinds enough that he could see inside.

The dining area was still dark. Through the service window, he could see light in the kitchen and somebody moving around. Female. But definitely shorter and heavier than Tara.

Not that he was looking for her.

He debated returning to his car to wait, but liking the stillness of the early morning, he merely leaned his back against the building. He'd barely taken three deep breaths when an old man walked around the corner.

"Morning," the man said. He stuck out a weathered, arthritic hand. "Nicholi Bochero."

Jake returned the shake. "Jake Vernelli."

"Figured as much. I live upstairs, above the restaurant. Got the lowdown on you last night from my grandson, Andy Hooper. The boy should be along shortly. He meets me for breakfast most mornings."

The door to the restaurant opened. The woman from the kitchen, wearing a white apron over her navy shirt and slacks, motioned them in. Her coarse gray hair was cut military-short and her face was lined with years of experience.

"Uh…morning, Janet. How…uh…are you?" Nicholi asked. The old man suddenly sounded out of breath.

"I'm all right, I guess," the woman answered. She turned away, but not before Jake saw a flush start at her neckline and spread its way north, filling in cracks and crevices. And like most cops who'd been cops for any length of time, he was pretty good at knowing when the energy in the air changed. In the past few seconds, it had skyrocketed upward.

Janet had Nicholi's coffee poured before the old man carefully lowered himself down on the second-to-last stool at the counter. He nodded his thanks and followed her movements with his eyes. Meanwhile Janet was looking everywhere but at him.

Oh, boy. Hormones—albeit some old ones—were shaking off some dust motes here. Jake slid in next to Nicholi, and when Janet held up the coffeepot in his direction, he nodded and practically sighed in appreciation when he took his first sip.

"New police chief?" Janet asked.

"Interim," Jake corrected immediately.

The door opened and Officer Hooper walked in. His face was freshly shaved and with his ruddy complexion, he looked about sixteen. "Morning, sir…uh…Chief," he said to Jake.

The kid made him feel ancient. "Morning, Andy."

The young officer walked past Jake, patted his grandfather gently on the back and took the last seat at the counter. "Where's Tara?" he asked.

"I don't know," Janet said. "When I arrived and she wasn't already here, I called her house. There was no answer, so I thought she must be on her way. However, if that's true, she should have been here at least fifteen minutes ago."

Jake tried to ignore the uneasy feeling in his

stomach but he couldn't shake the memory of the fear that he'd seen in Tara Thompson's eyes before she'd so carefully concealed it.

"She's never late," Andy said.

Nicholi unwrapped his silverware that had been rolled tight in a napkin. "You're right, son. Not even when we had two feet of snow in the middle of January."

Damn. Jake stood up and threw a buck on the counter. "You'll save my life if you put this in a to-go cup for me."

"You're going to go check on Tara?" Janet asked.

He nodded.

She shoved the dollar back toward him and filled a large paper cup with fresh coffee. "It's on the house."

A half mile out of town, Jake saw a bicycle on its side. He slowed down to take a closer look and saw a man squatted down in the shallow ditch. Jake slammed on his brakes, swung his car off to the shoulder and got out.

There was a woman lying on the ground. Jake saw strawberry-blond hair and scrambled down the steep embankment. He heard a noise behind him but didn't bother to look around. Andy Hooper had been following him since the edge of town.

The man was patting Tara's hand. Her eyes were closed and her head was tilted back slightly. She was holding a bloody handkerchief under her nose. Jake dropped to his knees.

"Tara," he said, his voice soft. "It's Jake Vernelli."

She opened her pretty green eyes and started to sit up. "I'm okay," she said, her voice muffled by the cloth.

Yeah, right. She had scratches on her legs and torn skin on her right knee. There were splotches of blood on her shirt that he hoped were from her nose. "Don't move," he said. Every cop knew some basic first aid. He reached for her wrist. Her pulse was strong and a little rapid but not horrible. He leaned closer and checked her pupils. Both the same. Both the right size.

"What injuries do you have?" he asked.

"Just scratches. Nothing much." She looked over his shoulder. "Hi, Andy."

"Thought you might need some backup, Chief," Andy explained. "You okay, Tara? You look like my dog did the last time he mixed it up with a coon."

Jake resisted the urge to rub out the pain that was gathering between his eyes. "What happened here?"

"I was running. A car coming toward me lost control, so I took the ditch."

She said it as if it was no big deal. Jake could feel the coffee churning in his empty stomach. He looked over his shoulder at the man. "Who are you?"

Tara sat up. She pulled the handkerchief away from her nose and set it aside, without looking at it. "Jake, this is Gordon Jasper. He's a good customer and was kind enough to loan me a handkerchief. Gordon, this is Jake Vernelli, our temporary police chief."

He nodded at Gordon. "Did you see what happened?"

"I'd just crested the hill on my bike and saw Tara running ahead of me. A car was coming toward us. There was nothing unusual until suddenly the car swerved toward Tara. From where I was, I thought she'd been hit. I have to tell you, it was a relief to find her in one piece when I got here."

Jake looked at Tara. "Did either of you get a license plate?"

"No," Tara said.

"Me either," Gordon added. "I got the hell off the road in case the idiot decided to take a swipe at me. I know it was white. A four-door. Maybe a Buick."

"Man or woman driving?" Jake asked.

Gordon shrugged. "Sorry."

Tara shook her head. Andy Hooper stood up. "It ain't much but I'll call it in. Maybe we'll get lucky."

Tara started to get up. He reached out a hand to help her, and after just the slightest hesitation she took it. Her touch was warm and soft, and he could feel his own heart start to beat a little fast. It jarred to a sudden stop when he saw the blood on the back of her head.

"Tara," he said, letting her hand go and reaching to brace her arm. "Slow down. You've got a head injury."

Her steps faltered. "I do?" She reached and patted her head. When she looked at her fingers and saw the blood on them, she turned white, and he was afraid she was going to faint.

He wrapped an arm around her. She felt fragile and vulnerable, and he wanted five minutes alone with the idiot who'd been too much of a damned coward to stop and help her. He stepped behind her and gently parted her hair. On the back of her skull, almost level with her ear, she had a bump and a small cut. There was quite a bit of blood, but he knew that head wounds bled more than almost any other part of the body. "It looks as if you might have sliced it on a rock. You're going to be fine," he said, wanting to reassure her. "The doctor may tell you that you don't even need stitches."

She turned to look at him. Her green eyes were big. "I'm not going to a doctor."

"You could have a concussion," he said. "You should be checked."

"No."

Hell. Scratch fragile and vulnerable. "Can I at least drive you home so that you can wash the blood off?" Once there, he'd take another look, and if he needed to, he'd throw her in the car and head for the nearest emergency room.

She swallowed hard. "That would be okay." She looked at Gordon. "Can we give you a lift?"

"No, thanks. Can't stand anything with an engine. Just glad to see you're okay." The two men, with Tara between them, walked up the hill. Jake kept his hand just inches away from her elbow, ready to catch her if she faltered.

Andy stood next to Jake's car. "Got a hold of Lori Mae. Officers in the surrounding four counties will be looking for the vehicle." He smiled at Tara. "I guess it's a good thing Chief Vernelli decided to look for you."

Tara stared at him. "Why did you do that?" she asked. Her tone wasn't as friendly.

He could hardly tell her that from the moment she'd answered the door last night and tried to rearrange some of his favorite parts with her knee, he'd been thinking about her. That would make him seem like some kind of nut. "I'm a cop. It's what we do."

It took a minute but finally she gave him a halfhearted smile. "I'm sorry," she said. "We started off on bad footing and I guess I haven't regained my balance yet."

Then they were even. He felt short of breath and a little light-headed himself. He opened the passenger door and motioned for Tara to sit. "Andy, I'll give Tara a lift home. Go have breakfast with your grandfather."

They drove the short distance to her house in silence. He barely had the car stopped before she opened the door and got out. He followed her up the steps and waited while she opened the screen door and unlocked the wooden door.

She turned. "Thank you."

He was being dismissed. And he didn't like it. She was pale and her hand wasn't quite steady. "Maybe I should come in. What if you fall over in the shower?"

"I won't."

Given that he'd already forced his way into her house once, he stepped back and sat down on the cement step. "If you're not out in fifteen minutes, all bets are off."

She chewed on her lower lip. "Fair enough." She pushed open the door. "Since you're going to be here and all, could you make sure nobody else comes in while I'm in the shower?" It was an offhand request, made casually. Too casually, perhaps.

"You're expecting someone?"

"No. But once Gordon gets to town, he might tell the story, and it wouldn't be that odd for someone to come out and check on me."

It sort of made sense. But there was something that wasn't right. "Okay. Nobody gets past me." He didn't miss the relief in her eyes before she turned away.

Chapter Four

Thirteen minutes later, she unlocked the door and came out onto the porch. She was dressed in a blue jean skirt that showed off her tanned, well-toned legs—the bandage on her knee and the fresh scratches couldn't even distract from their appeal. She wore a long-sleeved cotton shirt. She looked young and fresh and innocent, and it made him think that maybe he was crazy for suspecting that she was hiding something. His experience with Marcy had warped his judgment.

"Have a seat," he said, motioning to the step. He separated her silky hair to take a look at the cut. Her skin, her hair, something, smelled like raspberries and he was afraid to breathe too deep, afraid that it would be a scent that he wouldn't be able to easily shake.

The cut was a half-inch long. It had stopped bleeding and looked clean. "I think it's okay."

"Good." She stood up. "I need to get to work. Janet has got to be going crazy."

"While she and I didn't have much time to get acquainted, I got the impression that Janet is pretty competent. Couldn't she handle the place for a while so that you could rest?"

"I don't need to rest. And you're right. On a normal day, Janet could probably take care of the place with one hand tied behind her back. But we're short a dishwasher and, more important, tomorrow is the town picnic. The Chamber of Commerce provides the meat and pays Nel's to make the sandwiches. We've got over a hundred pounds of roast beef that needs to be cooked today so that we can slice it tomorrow for Italian beef sandwiches."

Town picnic. Chase must have been really worried about his mother to have forgotten to mention that. A hundred pounds of beef meant a lot of sandwiches. Which probably meant that a whole lot of people were expected. "So what happens at this event?"

"Everyone gathers for a parade. Then there's lunch in the park, some games for the kids, maybe some volleyball for the adults. By late afternoon, people drift off. There are lots of people in this community who still have milk cows, so they don't have the luxury of missing chores."

Cows. Chores. Town picnic. He was in the middle of a Norman Rockwell painting. All his debts to Chase were definitely going to be paid in full. He couldn't wait to get home to his apartment, where he knew his neighbors by sight but he sure as hell didn't spend any time talking to them.

"Any more thoughts about who might have been driving that car?" he asked.

"No."

"It strikes me as somewhat of a coincidence that you get a baseball through your window last night and this morning you're almost run off the road. Are you sure there's nobody pissed off at you?"

She stared at him. "Look, I appreciate the help. Both last night and this morning. But I can't imagine the two things have anything to do with one another. Last night was petty vandalism, and this morning it was an accident. The driver lost control, swerved, probably didn't even see me. Now I really have to be going."

Without another word, she walked to the garage and pulled her van out. When he motioned that he'd shut the garage door, she shook her head sharply, got out and did it herself. Then she waved her hand, making sure he understood that she expected him to leave first.

She couldn't have made it any clearer. *I don't need or want you watching over me.*

BY THE TIME Tara locked the restaurant's door that afternoon, she was almost shaking with fatigue. She wasn't surprised when she closed out the cash drawer that receipts were up almost twenty percent. The broken window had sparked plenty of interest, and by the time Gordon had told his tale around town, the lunch crowd had swelled to standing-room only.

Yes, I've got someone coming to fix the window.

Yes, I did take the ditch this morning.

I'm not sure either what this world is coming to.

Tara had refilled coffee cups and offered thick slices of strawberry rhubarb pie. One of her regulars offered her a dog. Said that he had a pit bull that could protect Nel's and her, but then again, maybe not, because he wasn't sure if the dog was a jogger.

Midafternoon, Janet had called her back to the kitchen because Chase Montgomery was on the phone. He'd expressed his concern about both the vandalism and the troubles on her morning run. Said that he'd spoken to Frank Johnson. She'd been touched that Chase had taken the time to call when clearly he had his own issues to deal with. She'd assured him she was fine and asked about his mom. "Tough days ahead" was all he'd said. He'd switched the topic quickly and had passed along the news that Chief Wilks was continuing to recover from his bypass surgery. That had led him to Jake.

"I'm grateful that Jake's there to take care of things. I don't know a better cop. Nothing gets past him."

The words had rattled around in her head for the

rest of the day. She needed supercop to look past *her,* to direct his attention on something else.

When she'd started imagining how convenient a bank robbery might be, she'd returned to the dining room and wiped off tables and trays and counters as if a health inspector had been spotted outside.

Now, hours later, she'd progressed from tired to truly exhausted. Her feet hurt and a dull pain had lodged itself in the middle of her back. The kitchen had been extra hot from the big ovens being on all day, making her shirt stick to her back and sweat gather between her breasts. When she cleaned the floor, the mop weighed a hundred pounds. To top it off, when she and Janet washed up the last of the pans, the normally taciturn woman surprised her by initiating conversation. Tara almost dropped the soup kettle on her foot.

"What do you think of the new police chief?" Janet asked.

"Seems nice," she said. She turned on the water and rinsed the large pan again. She grabbed a clean white towel and vigorously rubbed dry the dull stainless steel.

"He was Johnny-on-the-spot to go looking for you this morning."

And that had been nagging at her. In less than twelve hours, after Jake Vernelli had arrived in town, her business had been vandalized and she'd almost been killed. Could it really be as simple as just a streak of bad luck? Or had her luck truly run out? Had Michael found her? And was he somehow connected to the new police chief?

Nobody in Wyattville knew about Michael. When she'd first arrived in town, the trauma had been too fresh. Then, as her body healed and her mind cleared, she'd decided that the only way to protect herself was to make sure that no one, especially not the police who had betrayed her once before, could know the truth.

And up until now, it had been easy. Joanna Travis had vanished and Tara Thompson had appeared.

But Jake Vernelli made her nervous.

At midmorning, he'd shown up at the restaurant and had coffee with Frank Johnson. It had rattled her to have him at the counter. He'd watched her. Hadn't mentioned the accident again, but she'd known that every time another customer had asked about it, he'd listened to her answer.

Had he been trying to see if her story would change?

It hadn't. She'd told him the truth. The car had swerved, she'd reacted and hit the ground hard. The impact had stunned her, taken her breath away. She'd sat up as quickly as possible but by then the car was already over the next hill.

She'd caught only a glimpse of the driver before taking the ditch; he or she had worn a hat pulled low over the face. Maybe it had been an elderly person. Maybe someone coming home from third shift at the county hospital, and they'd fallen asleep and awakened at the last moment. There was no way to know if it had been Michael.

Michael Watson Masterly, the third. Of the New York Masterlys. Old money. Politically connected. Mean.

But she hadn't known any of that the night she'd met Michael at the governor's fundraiser. She'd been working. He'd been friendly and funny, and when he'd relentlessly pursued her for weeks afterward, she'd been naive enough to believe that she was living a fairy tale. Six months after they'd met, they were living together and she'd been planning their wedding. Three months later, she'd been running for her life.

If Jake Vernelli was working with Michael, then he'd stop at nothing short of killing her. If he wasn't, he was still dangerous. If he looked too close, he was going to see that her life was a house of cards, and she was only one pull away from having it collapse.

AT NINE THE NEXT MORNING, Tara wiped her face with a paper towel. On her way to work, she'd enjoyed the clear blue sky and brilliant sun. Now, just three hours later, the temperature outside had soared to ninety and was well over a hundred degrees in the kitchen.

The hottest summer in fifty-five years. The television weather forecasters droned on about it. In Minnesota, where summers for the most part lasted about two months and a hot day was in the mid-eighties, fourteen straight days of over ninety-degree temperatures had everyone's attention. People didn't talk about anything else.

Except for the past couple of days, they'd squeezed in a little conversation about the town picnic. Held every June fifteenth for the past hundred and ten years, the picnic brought the town together. Over five hundred people would gather at Washington Park, the two acres of land at the edge of Wyattville. Stories would be retold, recipes traded, new babies shown off and massive amounts of food consumed.

Since early morning, she and Janet had been slicing the meat they'd cooked the day before. The Lions Club would have three large roasters available to keep the meat warm so that it could be piled high onto fresh buns and topped with sautéed green peppers. Other volunteers would have fired up a few grills, and there'd soon be hot dogs and hamburgers sizzling. Each family that attended would bring a dish to pass. There would be lemonade and iced tea and big barrels of cold beer. No one would go away hungry.

The parade would mostly consist of tractors pulling hay wagons—decorated with crepe paper and plastic streamers—that could seat the mayor, city council members or anybody else remotely considered Somebody. Each would have a big bag of candy at his or her side, and they'd throw handfuls out along the way, and small children along the parade route would scramble for the loot.

Boy and Girl Scout troops would march, proudly carrying flags. Wyattville didn't have its own high school. Kids were bused to Bluemond, twenty-five miles away. The payback came at parade time when Bluemond's seventy-five-person band showed up. The parade started a block north of Nel's, so for the past half hour Tara had listened to a haphazard medley of blaring horns, whistling flutes and pounding drums as the kids nervously waited to begin marching.

At 10:45 a.m., fifteen minutes before the parade was to start, Tara locked the front door. Normally on a Friday, the last lunch special wouldn't be served until sometime around two but no one expected that today. Memorial Day, Fourth of July and Labor Day might be national holidays but in Wyattville, it was the town picnic that garnered universal observance.

Under one arm she carried two lawn chairs, one for her and one for Janet. The older woman had left a few minutes earlier to supervise sandwich making.

For most of the morning, Tara had been too

busy to worry about broken windows or hit-and-run drivers. Now that her work was done and the rest of the day stretched before her, she was determined not to dwell on what-ifs but rather to focus on sunshine, silly games and the simple pleasure of dangling her bare feet in the spring-fed pond.

At last year's picnic, she'd been so new and so edgy that the loud, unexpected burps of noise from the tractors had practically had her jumping out of her skin. Janet had been insistent, though, and she'd somehow managed to draw up her lawn chair and while away the afternoon hours with her new customers and neighbors. And looking back, she knew that was the day when the healing had started.

The people of Wyattville had opened their arms and their hearts, and she'd found a place to call home. Day by day, she'd gotten both mentally and physically stronger. She'd started sleeping at night and stopped her steady diet of antacid pills. The small town had healed her.

Tara stopped at the very edge of Washington Park and unfolded her lawn chair. She waved to several customers and they waved back. It wasn't until she'd sat down that she saw him.

Six feet of pure muscle. Before her nightmare with Michael began, she'd have appreciated this man's long legs, trim waist, broad chest. She might even have joked with coworkers about his fine rear end and speculated about other attributes. But now, with his pressed uniform, hat and shiny black shoes, he all but screamed cop, and it made her stomach cramp up in fear.

His stance was comfortable as he confronted a carload of teenagers who'd decided that the barricade across the road clearly didn't apply to them. But she wasn't fooled. He didn't carry himself like a cop who'd gotten soft working a desk and doing the occasional crowd control. No, definitely not. And he'd certainly handled his gun last night as if it was an extension of his arm.

Was it as simple as it all sounded? Had he really come to Wyattville to help his old friend? But who had the kind of job that they could just up and leave at any time for six weeks to go work somewhere else? No. There was more to the story.

And she loved a good story. Got jazzed piecing information together. There'd been few who were as good at re-creating a series of events that made sense.

Whether it was covering a political campaign, a murder trial or the transgressions of the big banks, she'd loved being a reporter. Loved seeing the results of her work on the newsstand. Loved the editorial deadlines, even loved the notoriously bad coffee in the break room.

But that was a long time ago. Now she needed to keep a low profile. She needed to stay out of Chief Vernelli's way and if she couldn't manage that, she needed to make darn sure that she was at the top of her game. She couldn't afford to slip up, to give him any reason to look at her closer.

She angled her chair, just enough that he was in her peripheral vision but not enough that he'd catch her eye. She bought a watery lemonade from two young girls and was relieved when the first floats came by. She was clapping for the Wyattville fire truck and volunteer fire department when a shadow blocked out the hot sun.

She twisted her body so quickly that one side of her lawn chair lifted off the ground, and she would have crashed to the side if a strong hand hadn't steadied her.

"Careful," he said.

"Chief Vernelli," she managed.

He glanced at the bandage on her knee. "Bumps and bruises getting better?"

She nodded and prayed that he'd move along. Instead, he spread his legs, shifted his weight back onto his heels, hooked his thumbs in the loops of his belt and watched the parade like it was Thanksgiving Day and he had a boatload of stock invested in Macy's.

She ignored him, and he appeared as if it didn't bother him in the least. When the funeral home director and his family rode by on a float decorated as a coffin, the crowd was peppered with wrapped caramels. Jake reached a long arm up and easily caught a piece. He tossed it in Tara's lap.

"It's your candy," Tara protested.

He shrugged. "I don't have much of a sweet tooth. I'd arm-wrestle you over a bag of potato chips, though."

More proof that he wasn't normal. She unwrapped the candy and popped it in her mouth as the last tractor belched and snorted its way past. Tara stood up and folded her lawn chair.

"What's next?" Jake asked.

I watch to see what direction you go in and make a mad dash in the other. "Lunch. Then we'll head for the shade and rest our stomachs until the games begin."

"I saw the dunk tank getting set up," he said.

"The chief of police would be a big draw," she suggested.

"Too bad I'm on duty." He smiled and she felt the answering lurch in her stomach. He was a handsome man. Might even be charming.

She edged away. "Given how hot it is, there will likely be plenty of volunteers. I may even try it myself." She turned and started walking. "I better hurry. Janet might need me," she lied.

FORTUNATELY FOR JAKE, Tara didn't get into the dunk tank. Breasts and cold beer were both good things. However, when the breasts were covered by a tight white T-shirt that suddenly became transparent, routine crowd control could quickly get ugly.

She did, however, play volleyball. Jake had stood off to the side, made small talk with those who wanted to get to know the new chief and discreetly watched the game. What Tara lacked in skill, she made up for in enthusiasm. Bending, stretching, lunging. She didn't do anything overtly over the top to attract attention, but when Jake scanned the crowd he saw several young men with their tongues almost hanging out.

Was it possible that her recent trouble had something to do with a rejected lover? He'd asked who she'd pissed off. Maybe the question should have been, *Who have you dumped lately?*

When the game ended, he watched to see who approached her. Several of the young men did, but with each she seemed casually comfortable. She didn't do much more than exchange a quick greeting with any of them until one too-thin, long-faced guy approached. He wore faded jeans and a white wife-beater T-shirt that revealed tattoos spread across both biceps. He was smoking a cigarette.

She looked surprised to see him. Then she motioned for the man to follow her, stopping when they were a distance from the volleyball court and anyone else who might hear the conversation. He talked, she mostly listened.

Then the man dropped his cigarette and with

more force than necessary, used the heel of his boot to grind it into the dirt. When Jake saw Tara frown, shake her head and turn away, only to be stopped by the man's hand on her arm, he moved fast.

"Problem?" he asked, when he reached Tara's side.

The man dropped his hand and stepped back.

"No. No problem," she said quickly.

He didn't buy it. "You two seemed to be having a pretty heated conversation," he said, staring at the man.

Tara stepped forward. "It was nothing," she said. She pushed her hair back from her face. "This is Donny Miso," she added. "Donny, Chief Vernelli."

The man didn't say anything and he stared at the ground. Close up, Jake could see that his hair was dirty, he hadn't shaved for a couple days and the dark circles under his eyes pointed to more than a few sleepless nights.

He looked a little desperate. And normally Jake had some sympathy for people who had reached the end of their rope. But he had no sympathy for a man who used his strength to dominate a woman, to force her.

"Donny, I think you better move on," he said.

"I don't want any trouble," Donny said.

"Then we want the same thing. Tara, I think Janet was looking for you. I'll walk you back that direction."

Without another word, Donny walked away. When he was almost out of sight, Jake turned to Tara. "Does he want his job back?"

"No. But the weird part is, he doesn't have anything else. I don't know what's going on with him. I think he's just so mad that his life isn't what he thought it was going to be. He probably needs counseling, but he couldn't afford to keep his health insurance after his real job ended. I'm worried about him."

"You think he could have had anything to do with the damage at the restaurant or with you being forced off the road yesterday?"

"I don't think he's mad at me. Just at life."

Even so, Jake made a mental note to have another conversation with Donny before the day ended.

"Excuse me," Tara said. "I need to find Janet."

She walked back toward the crowd and he waited several minutes before following. He found the women easily enough and wasn't surprised to see that Nicholi had managed to get his chair next to Janet's.

Tara had flopped down in the grass next to Nicholi's lawn chair, her legs stretched out in front of her, crossed at the ankles. Sand still clung to her tanned legs and bare feet. Her toenails were painted a bright red, and while he'd never considered himself to have a foot fetish, there was something incredibly sexy about her ten toes.

She leaned back on her arms, her head thrown back, her face raised to catch the sun. Jake pulled the collar of his shirt away from his throat and swallowed hard.

She was a perfect match to bright sunshine and blue skies. To sweet, juicy watermelon and ice-cold lemonade.

"How was the volleyball?" Nicholi asked.

"Exhausting. But I think I worked off your cheesy potatoes, Janet. Thank goodness Alice wasn't here with her cherry pie. Both would have done me in."

Nicholi put up a hand to shade his eyes from the bright sun. "I can't remember a year that Alice and Henry missed the town picnic."

Tara nodded. "I know. They left early yesterday to go see their son. Bill's getting married soon, you know."

Janet made some kind of grunting noise. "I wonder if Alice will finally be satisfied. She's been pushing that boy to get married for years. Lord knows she worked hard enough to match up the two of you."

Now that was interesting. Jake moved a step closer.

"Afternoon, Chief," Nicholi said.

Tara's eyes flew open and she jerked upright so fast that Jake thought she might have popped a vertebrae. But she was prevented from saying anything by the sudden arrival of Andy.

"Come on, Tara," the young man said. "It's time for the sack races. I need a partner."

She moaned. "Volleyball almost killed me."

"You've been saving potato sacks for months. You're the closest thing we have to a corporate sponsor."

The idea of her putting that sexy bare leg up against some other man's was unexpectedly revolting. Jake took another step forward. "I was hoping Tara would be my partner."

Chapter Five

"I couldn't," she said immediately. "Really." She stood up and took a step back. "I promised Andy."

Andy looked disappointed but held up his hands, clearly not wanting to piss off his new boss. "No problem, Chief. I'll find another partner. But when we beat the pants off the two of you, I'm hoping I don't get poisoned or fired."

Tara chewed on the corner of her upper lip. Then she took a breath and met his eyes. "Let's go," she said.

Without another word, she walked over to the starting line and held out a hand for a sack. He moved behind her but didn't speak. In the background, the Bluemond band played on. It appeared the kids were determined to provide a full afternoon's worth of entertainment. This was the third time he'd heard the same song. They'd shed their uniform jackets, their only concession to the heat.

She handed him the sack and he put one leg in. "If I die of a heart attack, promise me that you won't tell anyone that I died with one leg in a potato sack."

She shrugged. "You could die covered with yolk. The egg-tossing contest is next."

He rolled his eyes and barely managed to keep them from rolling back in his head when she stuck her long bare leg into the sack. Even through the fabric of his pants, he swore he could feel the softness of her skin. Her hip brushed against his, bone against bone.

"Ready?" she asked, her voice sharp.

"As ever," he said. He'd gotten himself into this situation, now he just needed to see it through. He inched his leg away, making space between them.

The whistle sounded, they hopped, almost fell, righted themselves, hopped again, and by the time they reached midway, had gotten into a rhythm. Ten feet from the finish line, he thought they had a chance of winning, but out of the corner of his eye he saw another couple catching up. He was so focused on them that he missed the pair on the other side who, instead of hopping, were lurching, like it was a damn long-jump competition. They overextended and would have crashed into Tara if Jake hadn't turned his body and swung her out of the way.

The momentum carried her into him, he fell, and before he knew it he was flat on his back. She was splayed on top of him, her face pressed flat into his neck, her breasts soft against his chest. His arms were wrapped around her, holding her tight. She was solid, yet delicate. Round in the right places. Smooth.

She moved, jerking her head up so fast that a long strand of silky strawberry-blond hair brushed his cheek. He inhaled sharply, and when his lungs filled with a burst of raspberry, he realized he'd made the mistake that he'd managed to avoid on her front steps. The scent would haunt him. No doubt about it.

She stared at him, the black pupils of her green eyes big and round. And he suddenly couldn't hear a thing—not the band, not the crowd—all he could hear was the sound of her uneven breath. Her lips were parted and he knew that all he needed to do was lift his head and he'd be kissing her. He—

"Tara, are you okay?" Andy was there, squatting down next to them. When he offered a helping hand, Tara grabbed it quickly, and scrambled out of the potato sack. Andy offered a hand to Jake, but Jake waved it away. He got up more slowly, feeling oddly off balance.

"You guys would have won," Andy said.

"It was a good effort," Jake said. He looked at Tara, but she was busy dusting some invisible grass off her shorts. "I hope you didn't add to your collection of bruises," he said.

She shook her head. "I'm fine. No harm done."

Did she really believe that? Because his brain felt pretty scrambled.

"Gonna do the egg toss?" Andy asked.

Speaking of scrambled. "No. I think I'll sit this one out." He turned and set off through the crowd. One pass-through convinced him that the most dangerous thing happening was that Lori Mae's seven-year-old twin boys, Riley and Keller, who he'd met just briefly yesterday when they'd come to the station to meet their mom for lunch, were perched high in a tree spitting watermelon seeds at unsuspecting souls.

He pretended he didn't see them but figured they had seen him when he heard a gasp and leaves rustling. He hoped one of them didn't fall and break a leg. He didn't want to have to explain that to their mother. Lori Mae had spent an hour with him yesterday, helping him orient to the job. She'd been especially helpful in filling in the details about the picnic. She was mid-thirties and had married her high school sweetheart twelve years ago. He was currently serving his second tour in the Middle East. She appeared to run the department without missing a beat. She worked eight to five, Monday through Friday. When she went home at night and on the weekends, the phones were switched over to the county dispatch center.

He figured she was close by, and sure enough, she was standing next to Nicholi and Janet, who were still resting in their lawn chairs. Jake walked over and leaned up against the tree behind them. Everyone's attention was on the egg tossing contest that was about to start.

Tara and Andy were lined up across from one another, about ten feet apart. After each successful toss, each of the participants had to take a step backward. By the time it got down to the final three couples, Andy and Tara were a good thirty feet apart and fiercely concentrating.

Next toss, Tara to Andy. Her throw might have been a little high, but Andy was a beanpole and he was able to reach it. He grinned like a little kid and Tara clapped her hands. One step back for each.

Andy made a big production out of his windup. He was just about to let loose when a saxophone started playing. Jake couldn't locate the source, but it was faint enough that he figured it was a band member walking home, not yet ready to give up the fight.

The egg left Andy's hand and Tara—well, Tara was searching the crowd, her eyes moving frantically. The egg hit Tara's shoulder and splattered.

Andy came running across the grass toward her. "Tara, you weren't even looking," he said.

"I'm…I'm sorry, Andy."

Jake was close enough that he could see that all the color had drained from her face and that her hand, when she picked the shell off her shirt, was trembling.

Jake glanced around the crowd, didn't see anything out of place, nothing that would have caused that kind of reaction. He noted that the sax had stopped.

"That's why I don't do the egg toss," Lori Mae said. Both Nicholi and Janet smiled in response.

Jake watched as the contest finished out. Andy and Tara congratulated the winners and then wandered over to join the group. Andy flashed a grin at Jake. "Hey, Chief. I'm going to take off now. My shift starts in just a few minutes. I'll change at the station."

Jake nodded absently. Tara was still far too pale.

"Honey," Janet said, "your shirt is a mess."

Tara looked down, as if finally seeing it. "Mostly on my sleeve," she said softly.

Which caused Jake to take a second glance. Earlier he'd been so busy looking at her legs that he hadn't focused on the fact that she had on a long-sleeved T-shirt. Granted, it was a very lightweight shirt but still, it was over ninety degrees. It reminded him that even when she'd been running, she'd had on a long-sleeved shirt. What the hell?

Drugs? Were her arms covered with track marks?

Maybe. But if so, she was the healthiest-looking user he'd ever seen. He wasn't normally a betting man, but he'd bet the farm that she was clean. But why the modesty?

Lori Mae stood up. "I better go find my two little hooligans and get them home."

"Second tree on your left," Jake said.

"Thanks, Chief. So what did you think of your first Wyattville picnic?"

First and last. He'd be gone by the end of summer, and he wasn't likely to be back this direction. But it hadn't been as bad as he'd expected. He'd thought it would be corny and tedious, and while there had been moments of both, there'd been something genuinely nice about watching a community gather for something as simple as shared food and conversation.

In the city, there were festivals where crowds gathered, but it was because there was a shared interest in the event, not a shared interest in each other. That was what made this different.

"It was a pleasure," Jake said honestly.

Nicholi stood up, got his balance and carefully folded his lawn chair. "By the way, I spoke with Chase Montgomery today. Unfortunately, his mother's recovery may take longer than expected. He's thankful you're here. Said he'd trust you with his life and that we were lucky to have you."

Everyone was looking at him, waiting for him to say something, perhaps to explain why he'd come to Wyattville. Jake could feel the warmth in his face and he knew it had nothing to do with the sun. What could he say? *I screwed up, my partner almost killed me, and I'm not sure I can be a cop anymore.* Yeah. That would inspire confidence. "He's a good man," he said finally.

Lori Mae studied him and he realized that he might have his hands full with her. But she didn't push. Just said a general "Good night everyone," and walked away.

"I better get going, too," Tara said. "Do you want me to help you carry your chairs?" she added, looking at Janet.

"I've got them," Nicholi said.

Tara didn't argue. Jake realized she wasn't about to take away the man's pride. "Okay. Good night."

She'd barely gone twenty yards when Nicholi said, "I just love that girl. She's been a breath of fresh air in Wyattville."

"Hopefully her streak of bad luck is over," Janet said. "First the broken window and then run off the road by a crazy driver. She's due for some good luck."

Jake didn't believe in luck. Good or bad. He didn't believe in coincidence. He believed actions caused reactions. Push and push back kept the universe in balance.

Somebody or something was pushing at Tara. And he was going to figure out what it was.

TARA HAD STOPPED SHAKING by the time she got home. Damn it. She'd heard that saxophone, recognized the song as one that Michael favored, and freaked. She was lucky the egg hadn't caught her square in the face.

It was a popular song, one that most everybody knew. It meant nothing that she'd heard it today, just days after other crazy stuff happened. Meant nothing that it was a saxophone, Michael's favorite instrument.

Right?

There was such a thing as being hypersensitive. Neurotic. Crazy, even.

She needed to keep her perspective—to not see monsters under the bed, or in the closet, or at the town picnic for goodness' sake. She made a sharp right into her driveway and told herself that it wasn't nutty to slow down and assess her surroundings, to take an extra few seconds to make sure that nothing was out of place. It was smart. Sensible.

She parked, not bothering with the garage. Once she got cleaned up she needed to run to the grocery store. She winced getting out of the van, knowing that her muscles would probably hurt even more the next day. She slung her purse over her shoulder and was halfway to the house before she saw it.

She took one more foolish step forward before turning and running for her van. She fumbled with her keys, wasting seconds before she got the vehicle started. Throwing it in Reverse, she backed out, turned the wheel sharply and peeled out of her driveway, all the time keeping her eyes on the rearview mirror.

She was halfway to town before she remembered to breathe. She took a big gulp of air, hoping to calm her nerves and jump-start her brain.

Her stomach tight with dread, she drove to the small brick building at the edge of town that housed police, volunteer fire and the city clerk's office in different sections.

She opened the door to the police department and walked into an empty room. At the rear of the room, the door to the small bathroom was open and the light was off. Where the heck was he?

"Andy?" she yelled.

Jake Vernelli strolled out of the back room, carrying a manila file folder. He wasn't smiling.

"What are you doing here?" she blurted out.

He tilted his head down. "I thought we'd covered that. I work here."

She swallowed nervously. "I'm sorry. I didn't mean it that way. I was expecting Andy."

He raised an eyebrow. "And was he expecting you? Exactly what are the good citizens of Wyattville spending their tax dollars on?"

She got the implied message. "Don't be ridiculous," she snapped. "He left the picnic because his shift was starting." She drew in a deep breath and fought for control. "Never mind. I'm sorry to have bothered you."

He got to the door before she did. "Andy apparently ate a few too many hot dogs today. I understand he became indisposed on his way here. He called me and I told him I'd cover."

She tried to step around him, but once again he moved fast and stayed between her and the door.

"What's going on?" he asked. "You look as if you're about to fall over."

Tara didn't want to tell him. She didn't trust him. But Chase Montgomery trusted him, and he was no fool. And one thing was certain—Jake had been at the picnic all day. His whereabouts were accounted for.

Who else could she turn to? If it was Michael, then she'd need someone who could handle him. Someone faster, tougher.

"I need some help," she said. "Someone broke into my house today." Tara's legs felt weak, like she'd done ten flights of stairs. She walked over to the worn, faded office chair and sank down.

"Tara?" Jake prompted. He walked close to her chair. She kept her head down, staring at his black shoes. It was so tempting to ignore what had brought her back to town. All she'd done since Jake Vernelli had arrived in town was attract attention.

Why on earth would she give him one more reason to wonder about her?

Because to do anything else would be careless. Stupid really. She needed to deal with what was happening at her house before it dealt with her. She tilted her head up and made eye contact. "When I got home after the picnic, I realized that someone had been in my house. Or maybe—" she swallowed hard "—*is* still inside? I don't know."

Jake's brown eyes were bright, alert, already processing. "You didn't see anybody?"

"No."

"And you didn't go inside?"

"No."

"Was your door bashed in?"

"No."

"Tara?" Jake scratched his head. "Then just how do you know that somebody broke in?"

"My screen door doesn't latch. When you go through it, it partially closes but it never latches. You have to make an effort to pull the door and then turn it just so, so that it stays latched. The tension is wrong," she explained.

He didn't say anything but she could tell by the skeptical look on his face that he wasn't convinced.

"I always latch my screen door. I check and double-check that, too. When I got home tonight, it was unlatched."

Jake rubbed his jaw. "Tara, you no doubt left

your house in a hurry this morning. You probably didn't latch it."

"I didn't use that door this morning. I used my back door. I know the front door was latched. I know it," she repeated. "I don't forget details." Not when her life might depend on it.

Jake stayed silent. "Okay," he responded finally. "I'll go take a look." He reached for his keys on the desk and took two steps toward the door. He stopped and sighed. "You're not going to stay here, are you?"

She shook her head.

"I didn't think so. Just please don't get out of your vehicle when we get to your house."

JAKE STOPPED HIS CAR two hundred feet shy of her driveway. He pulled off onto the side of the gravel road. She pulled in behind him.

He got out and walked back to her van. "I need your house key."

She pulled it off the ring. "This one unlocks both the door lock and the bolt lock. Front and back doors are keyed the same."

"Okay. I'll check it out. You stay here," he said.

Tara didn't answer.

"Tara, you will stay in this car, won't you?" he asked.

She nodded. What choice did she have? Her legs

were shaking so much that she doubted they would hold her.

The trees on the property were thick enough to offer cover for her car but sparse enough that she could still see him after he'd walked up the road and made the turn into her driveway. For a big man, he moved quietly. His right arm was raised, bent at the elbow, the barrel of the gun pointed at the sky.

Using his foot, he eased open the still-unlatched screen door. He pushed his foot against the wooden door but nothing happened. She waited for him to try the key but he didn't. Instead, he backed away from the house and down the steps. Then, his body hugging the foundation, he edged around her small house.

When he disappeared from sight, Tara sucked in a deep breath. *One one hundred. Two one hundred. Three one hundred.* When she got to twenty, she gave up all pretense of waiting patiently.

She opened her door, cringing when it made a soft squeak. She moved cautiously up the length of driveway and across her small yard, sure she would be shot at any moment.

She was five feet from her front door when it swung open. There was a shadow of a man and Tara caught the glimpse of a gun.

"It's me," she squeaked.

It was more of a hiss than a sigh. "I told you to stay in the van."

"I know. Is everything okay?" she whispered.

"There's nobody inside. You can come in."

She walked past him but stopped no more than three feet into the house. The heavy drapes were all closed, making it seem as if the daylight had suddenly disappeared. Jake flipped on the light switches in both the kitchen and the living room. She sank down on the couch.

"Are you all right?" Jake asked, crouching in front of her. "You're still pretty pale."

If he were lucky, she wouldn't vomit on his shoes.

"I checked the bedroom and the bath," he said. "Everything seems to be in order. The doors were locked, Tara. Both doors, both locks."

So no one had been in her house. That was the easy explanation. She was crazy.

Except that she wasn't. Her house felt different. The rug in front of the door seemed slightly out of place. The drawer of the corner desk was almost closed, as if someone had hurriedly brushed a hand toward it but hadn't taken the time to make sure it was shut tight. Like she would have.

"Do you still think somebody was inside?" Jake asked.

She felt old and brittle and desperately wanted to scream. But she needed to be very careful. The ability to move quickly, without anyone expecting her to do so, was what had saved her once before. If anyone knew she was spooked, she'd lose that element of surprise and that could prove deadly.

Chapter Six

She forced a smile. "I'm sorry I brought you out here on a wild-goose chase."

Jake shook his head. "No problem. Does anybody besides you have a key?"

Her turn to shake her head.

"No ex-boyfriends?" he asked. For the first time, his gaze wasn't meeting her eyes. He was staring somewhere above her head.

"I don't give keys to men that I date."

"Even Bill Fenton?" He shrugged. "I couldn't help overhearing the conversation at the picnic."

Right. He saw and heard too much. That was what made him so dangerous. "Last year, Bill was living with Alice and Henry and he spent a lot of time drinking coffee at Nel's. He was between jobs and probably bored."

"You never went out?" he asked.

"One time we went to the Big Dip and got ice cream cones. I think—" she hesitated "—it is possible that he might have exaggerated our relationship.

When he left town suddenly, I got the impression from Alice that she thought I might have had something to do with his sudden departure. I didn't know if Bill inadvertently or purposefully misled her. I hoped it would blow over, and it must have because Alice hasn't mentioned it lately."

"So Alice and Henry must have a key?"

"Yes."

"Maybe they stopped by?"

It was possible but they weren't expected back until tomorrow. "Maybe," she agreed.

"Or maybe somebody else stopped by, knocked, realized you weren't home and then left. But they didn't realize they needed to latch the screen door."

"You're probably right." There were a thousand reasonable explanations. They could play this game all day.

Jake stared at her. Then he sat down on the chair opposite the couch. He looked very serious. The irony didn't escape her. They were in the same positions they'd been that first night he'd come to her home. He'd looked very serious that night, too.

"Anything you want to tell me, Tara?" he asked.

Damn. "No. I mean, thank you. I appreciate your help. You must have a hundred things to do. I mean, being new and all. I'm sure you need to get back."

He shook his head. "No. I got a text from Andy. He's feeling much better and will finish out the shift. I'm done for the day."

This was getting worse by the minute. "I imagine you're pretty tired. Hot day in the sun and all."

He looked around her kitchen. "I wouldn't turn down a cup of coffee."

Act like a normal person. Did she even remember what that was like? "Of course."

Tara ran the water and filled the pot, making sure she only made enough for one cup for each of them. She fiddled around, putting away the clean dishes that had dried in the rack next to the sink. Then she pulled out the silverware drawer and did the same with the utensils, carefully stacking each fork and spoon. She wiped down an already clean counter.

When the coffee was done brewing, she poured one for herself and a second cup for Jake. *Act like a normal person.* It was going to become her new mantra. *Act normal, people will think you're normal, and if you're really lucky you'll start to believe it yourself. You'll forget that normal ended fourteen months ago.*

"So what did you think of the picnic?" she asked.

"First time I ever saw a tractor with streamers hanging off it," he said. "I've seen them in the field while I was driving down the highway. They're a lot bigger close up and fancier, too. Heck, I think the one had a fully stocked bar and a couch inside the cab."

She smiled, remembering how shocked she'd been when she'd first seen the farm equipment.

"Maybe not a couch but definitely a small refrigerator, GPS and a soft chair."

"Sounds like my apartment in Minneapolis without the GPS."

"Have you always lived in the city?" It surprised her that she wasn't simply going through the motions of small talk. She wanted to know.

"Yes. Born and raised. Only time I ever left was when I enlisted in the Marines."

"How old were you?"

"Nineteen. I'd been inspired by Operation Desert Storm. Never got to Iraq, but at one point I ended up in Somalia, where a peacekeeping, rebuilding effort went bad and I almost got my butt kicked."

She'd interviewed a number of veterans over the years. The things they had seen always amazed her. "Was it horrible?"

"Some of it. But a lot of it was very good. It changed my life."

"How? Why?" The questions were out of her mouth before she could stop them.

He laughed. "You're not from the *National Enquirer* or anything, are you?"

Yikes. She needed to be more careful. "I'm just curious. If you'd rather not say..."

He shook his head. "I got married right out of high school. Wendy and I were both eighteen. She was two months pregnant."

He had a wife. A child. Maybe more than one.

Her reporter's intuition had rarely failed her so completely. "I didn't realize you were married." *My gosh, my voice sounds stiff.*

"Wendy miscarried at four months. We got divorced a year later."

Her heart broke for the loss he suffered when he was barely a man himself. "I'm sorry, Jake. The death of a child is probably really hard for a couple to manage."

"Yeah, well, I was willing to try. I had this crazy idea that marriage was for life. But it was tough. We had jobs but we were making minimum wage, barely making ends meet."

"What happened?"

"Less than a year later she was pregnant again." He stood up and walked into the kitchen. He had his back to her.

"You didn't want the baby?" she asked.

It was several seconds before he turned, facing her once again. "I'm sorry," he said. "I don't talk about it much. Wendy and I hadn't slept together for three months, so I knew the baby wasn't mine. The father ended up being the manager of the local ten-minute oil-change shop. He was forty, more than twice as old as we were. He had a house, a boat, his ends were meeting."

He said it calmly, without emotion, but she could tell the hurt had never really gone away. "What did you do?"

"Signed the divorce papers and left. Hell, I didn't really blame her. I was going nowhere. I didn't have any education. What was I going to be able to offer her? So I enlisted in the Marines. That's when I realized I'd skipped college but somehow managed to join the let's-kick-their-asses fraternity."

"You make it sound almost fun."

"War is never fun. But the Marines taught me self-discipline. They taught me respect for authority. They taught me that the difference between life and death, the difference between coming home whole or in a pine box, can be just a couple inches. They taught me how to be a man."

He wasn't giving himself enough credit. He'd accepted a man's responsibilities at the age of eighteen, long before he'd become a marine.

"You came home," she said, stating the obvious.

"Yeah. Although I still didn't have a job or an education and my family was a mess. My parents were separated, my younger brother was a suicidal drunk."

"What happened while you were gone?"

"Sam is just a year younger than me. He'd always been the student of the family. He got an academic scholarship to Northwestern, a pretty swanky private school in Chicago. Great journalism program. He swung an internship at the *Chicago Tribune,* and all he talked about was working there after graduation."

Friends from school had gone to work at Mother Tribune, the flagship of the Tribune enterprises. She had visited them just months before she'd run from D.C. Michael would have contacted them, looking for her. Who knew what kind of crazy story he'd told them about why she'd left? He sure as heck wouldn't have told them the truth.

"While I'd taken a local train, with lots of stops and starts and getting-off points, Sam was on the express, in full pursuit of the American Dream."

"But something happened to derail him?"

"Yeah. His fiancée got murdered. He found her. Her skull had been bashed in." Jake's voice had turned hard and his jaw looked stiff. "Even worse, for a while, he was the prime suspect."

"Oh, my." It seemed inadequate, but it was all she could think of to say. Even after all these years the pain was evident in his voice, and she knew that Jake Vernelli had suffered for his brother.

"I'm sorry. It must have been a horrible time."

"Something like that changes a person. It changes the people who love that person."

She understood that. Violence had changed her.

"Is that why your parents had trouble?"

"Evidently before I got home, Sam had been spinning out of control for a while. My parents didn't know what to do. My mom made excuses and my dad thought tough love was the answer. They fought about it constantly. I think they were both just scared that they weren't going to be able to pull Sam back from the edge. It got so bad that they separated."

His family had fallen apart. "Not exactly the Welcome Home party you were expecting?"

He shrugged and gave her a half smile. "Not really. But I got my brother sobered up, worked full-time and went to school full-time."

"You make it sound easy but I'm betting it wasn't."

"You spend enough hours burrowed into the ground during a sandstorm and you get your priorities in line."

"What happened with your parents?"

This time it was a full smile that reached his dark eyes. "They got back together. If it weren't for them, I'd probably think all marriages were hopeless. But they showed that love can endure."

"But yet you never got married again?" She was sorry the minute she asked the question. It was too personal and what did it matter anyway. "Never mind," she said, holding up the palm of her hand.

He shook his head. "It's okay. Fourteen months of wedded bliss at the age of eighteen didn't scar me for life. Maybe someday, if I find the right woman, and I know she's not going to lie to me, then, who knows?" He rinsed his now-empty coffee cup in the sink and placed it on the drying rack. Then he took two steps toward the door before turning suddenly.

"You ever been married?" he asked.

She *was* scarred—both literally and figuratively. "No."

"Not even close?"

It was the perfect opportunity. She could tell him the truth. But he was a cop. Had worked hard to become one. How could she expect him to look the other direction?

She worked hard on her own smile. "Not even."

He rapped his knuckles on the wood door frame. "Here's hoping you have better luck than I did. I'm going to take off. Will you be okay?"

"Absolutely." She watched him walk through the front door. Then she got up, locked both the door lock and the bolt lock, and then sank into the nearest chair. *If I find the right woman and I know she's not going to lie to me.*

She'd done more than just lie *to him.* Her whole life was a lie. Tara Thompson was real. She just wasn't really Tara Thompson.

THE NEXT MORNING, Tara drove to town at a more normal speed than she had the previous evening. It was not yet six but already light when she turned into the small parking lot behind the restaurant. As she did every morning, she took a minute to cast a quick look around, making sure that nobody was waiting for her. With her keys in her hand, she walked to the door, quickly unlocked it and pulled it shut behind her.

She lit the grill first and then started the coffee brewing. She walked into the cooler and pulled out flats of eggs. The next trip in, she grabbed the boxes of bacon and sausage that Janet would fry up once she arrived. Within fifteen minutes, she'd mixed up the dough for biscuits. She'd never even had biscuits and gravy until she'd arrived in Minnesota. She and her friends in D.C. had been more the poached-egg-on-toast types.

"Morning."

Tara jumped, almost knocking a bowl off the counter. She hadn't heard the back door. "Good morning, Janet. I guess we both survived the picnic. Thanks again for your help."

"Nice event. Pretty warm, though."

"Yes. I'm grateful that we don't have to turn the ovens on today to cook roast beef. They say it may reach a hundred degrees." She rested her spoon on the butcher-block table. "I'll let you take over here. I'm going to go flip the sign."

As she unlocked the door, she smiled as Nicholi came in, folded newspaper under one arm. He made a point to wave to Janet in the kitchen, who gave him a curt nod in return. Tara poured a cup of coffee and set it in front of him. He added one creamer and a half a packet of sugar, just like he did every other morning.

The door opened and Toby Wilson walked in, taking the next seat at the counter. In addition to the pie he ate every day, he also put away a big breakfast every morning. "The usual, Toby?" Tara asked. The man ate two eggs, sunny-side up, with bacon, fried potatoes and toast every day. Her cholesterol had probably gone up just from carrying his plate.

"Wait a minute on putting the order in," he said, stirring the coffee Tara poured. "Chief Vernelli is supposed to meet me here."

Tara knocked the coffeepot against the counter and hot liquid splashed onto her hand.

Nicholi frowned at her. "Better be careful," he said.

He didn't know the half of it. "Just let me know when you're ready," she said. She put the coffee back on the burner and turned to escape to the kitchen.

She got two steps before she heard the door open. Looking over her shoulder, she saw Andy Hooper and Jake Vernelli walk in. Andy sat next to his grandfather. Jake took the stool next to Toby. His hair was still damp from his shower and his skin, which had looked red the day before from his time in the sun, had already turned to a deep tan. His shirt was stretched across his broad shoulders and his cop belt rested nicely on his hips. In food terms, he was a prime cut. Well-seasoned.

And probably just as addicting as a turtle cheesecake. Which she had also been known to crave from time to time.

"Coffee?" she asked, and was immediately grateful that she sounded almost normal.

"Is the Pope Catholic?" Jake asked.

That set Nicholi and Toby off. They laughed like little kids who'd gotten their feet tickled.

Tara rolled her eyes and Jake smiled. "How's my truck?" he asked Toby.

"Besides having a good-sized dent in the right fender and a busted-out windshield, she's a beauty. The glass for the window is coming today, and I got my best guy already working on the dent. Another day or so, she'll be back to good as new."

Andy leaned around his grandfather. "Toby, why do you always refer to vehicles as *she*s?"

"Because they can be temperamental and expensive and sometimes even difficult to start, but every man still wants one."

It was an old joke but it set Nicholi and Toby off again, with Andy joining in. Jake continued to sip his coffee, looking at her over the rim of his cup.

With a good-natured smile, Tara refilled all the coffee cups. "When you all get done amusing yourselves," she said, "I'll be happy to take your orders."

"I'm ready," Jake said.

She pulled an order pad out of the pocket of her khaki skirt. "Pancakes and bacon. By the way," he added, his voice much lower, "after I left your house last night, I had a conversation with Donny Miso."

"Why?"

"He left the picnic just before the egg toss. I wanted to know what he did after that."

Donny didn't have any reason to harm her. Heck, she'd even paid him cash just to help him out. If she'd paid him by check he'd have lost his unemployment benefits. The guy was down and out on his luck. She knew what that felt like.

"And?" she prompted.

"I found him at the Double-Pull Tap. Evidently he likes his lemonade with some vodka mixed in. He'd had a few before I talked with him. Said he'd come straight from the picnic. Bartender vouched that he'd been there since about the time I saw him leave. He wasn't at your house."

"I hope you didn't scare him. He seems pretty fragile right now."

"The man is a drunk. You're better off without him."

She didn't think so. Donny probably did drink too much and he'd been acting erratic lately, but still, she needed a dishwasher. And Donny had left a message on her voice mail just that morning, asking if he could come by that afternoon.

THREE HOURS LATER, Tara was stirring the cream of broccoli soup when Alice Fenton popped back into the kitchen. The woman who had been first her landlord, then her friend, wore a flannel shirt, blue jeans and scuffed loafers. She was four inches taller than Tara and probably carried another thirty pounds, making her an imposing figure, even at the age of sixty. Her face was lined, but her eyes were still clear and sharp. Not for the first time, Tara wished it could have worked out between her and Bill. Alice would have been a great mother-in-law.

"Nice plywood on your door window," Alice said. She hugged Tara and ignored Janet, who stood at the grill making the last of the day's pancakes before they switched over to lunch. Janet turned slightly, so that her back was to Alice.

Tara didn't expect any different. She knew there was no love lost between the two women—they'd had an argument some fifteen or twenty years earlier and neither seemed inclined to put it in the past. Janet had a son about the same age as Bill Fenton, and Tara thought the issue had something to do with the two boys.

Shortly after arriving in Wyattville and seeing the animosity, she'd discreetly tried to get the details. Neither had been forthcoming, and it drove her crazy that the two people she cared about most in Wyattville couldn't stand each other. She'd contemplated asking someone else about it but hadn't wanted either Alice or Janet to think that she was stirring up gossip about them.

"Welcome back," Tara said. Fifteen minutes earlier, through the service window, she'd caught a glimpse of Alice and Henry in the dining room and had assumed the woman would make a beeline back to the kitchen at her first opportunity. Henry, knowing he'd get the lowdown from Alice on the way home, had stayed in the dining room, talking with other farmers.

"You should have called us before we went out of town that morning to see Bill. We would have stopped in to help you clean up the mess."

It wasn't an empty promise. Over the past fourteen months, Alice and Henry had both been very helpful. When the dish machine had sprung a leak, Alice had made sure that Henry was there to fix it. And when rain had soaked through the roof, and then through the ceiling tiles, leaving puddles throughout the restaurant, Alice had been on her hands and knees, right alongside Tara, mopping up the mess.

"What exactly happened?" Alice asked.

She had no doubt heard a couple versions by now. One of the few negatives about Alice was that she liked to gossip. In her favor, she did try to have her facts straight.

"Some kid was sharpening up his throwing arm," Tara said.

"Is that what the police say?" Alice picked up a tomato and squeezed. Evidently it met inspection because she put it next to the others waiting to be sliced.

"Yes," Tara replied. "That's the only reasonable explanation." Of course, they didn't realize that Michael Masterly didn't have a reasonable bone in his body. Irrational. Temperamental. Judgmental. Those were all better adjectives. And he was a master at hiding it.

She shifted over and stirred the sauce that was bubbling in the large pan on the burner next to the soup. Today's special was spaghetti and meatballs. Janet's parents had brought the recipe with them from the old country, and Tara had almost passed out from pleasure the first time she'd tasted the dish. She wasn't the least bit offended that Janet didn't trust her to do anything but stir.

"That teenage hoodlum should have to pay to replace the window," Alice said.

"The window is getting fixed this afternoon. But maybe *the hoodlum,*" she said, winking at Alice, "could mop my floor for a month. That would be a nice trade-off."

"I heard the new interim police chief helped you clean up the mess that night. What's he like?"

Decisive. Maybe even bossy. Sexy as heck. "He's a big-city cop who is helping out an old friend. I get the feeling that the pace here is a little slower than what he's used to."

"I thought I might have him over for dinner. With Chase gone, the man is probably knocking around in that empty house. And I thought it might be a nice opportunity for him to meet Madeline."

Now, that made more sense. Bill's twin had moved home after her divorce last year. For a couple months, both adult children had been living in the house with their parents. Based on a few of Bill's comments, Tara had always thought he sought refuge at Nel's to avoid Madeline.

For Alice and Henry's sake, Tara had tried on several occasions to have a conversation with Madeline but the woman hadn't given her the time of day. Alice wasn't the only person who gossiped in Wyattville, and Tara had heard several versions of Madeline's latest exploits with a married man who lived just outside of town.

Madeline liked men. Tara bet she'd really like Jake. "Matchmaking?" she asked, trying hard to keep her tone light. The idea of Madeline getting her claws into Jake was disturbing.

"What if I am? But I'd like you to come, too."

The spoon slipped out of Tara's hand and sank in the heavy sauce. Janet turned to look at her—she was frowning. Tara hastily grabbed some tongs and used them to fish the spoon out. All the while, her brain was scrambling to think up a way to refuse. Was she really expected to watch Madeline flirt with Jake all night? Unfortunately Alice didn't take *no* well. That might also have been what led Bill to hide out at Nel's.

"I'm pretty busy here, Alice. And I've got a stack of paperwork to go through."

"Nonsense. You need to eat. And I don't want it to be too obvious, you know. Please."

Act normal. She couldn't make this a bigger deal than it needed to be. And Alice had helped her so many times. "Okay. Just tell me when."

"Tonight. I already stopped at the police station and he's available. I took the liberty of telling him that you'd be joining us. We'll eat around seven."

It took everything Tara had to keep a smile on her face. "Great. See you tonight."

The woman was almost out of the kitchen when Tara stopped her. "Hey, Alice, did you and Henry happen to stop by my house late yesterday afternoon?"

"Why?" Alice asked. Her neighbor appeared a bit startled, and Tara wondered if she'd been too abrupt in switching topics.

"When I got home after the picnic last night, my front screen door wasn't closed. The latch doesn't catch quite right. I thought maybe you'd needed to come inside for something. I know Henry has some old tools in the basement still."

Alice smiled. “Honey, we didn’t get back into town until late.”

“That’s what I thought. Never mind, then.”

“I’ll just have to make sure Henry gets that door fixed for you.”

“No problem.” She didn’t want the door fixed. She needed all the early warning signals she could find.

Chapter Seven

Jake cruised through Wyattville. It didn't take long. Main Street was less than three blocks long. There was Nel's, Frank Johnson's drugstore, a hardware store, a resale clothing store, another restaurant about the size of Nel's, Chase's law office, a bank, a decent-sized grocery store, the Double-Pull and a smaller bar. Flanking each end of town was a church. If you were Catholic, you headed south. The Methodists went north.

If you needed a doctor, a dentist or an accountant, you drove to Bluemond. There was a smattering of retail on the side streets, mixed in with residential housing. A day-care center, a tailor, a couple gas stations and a psychic. He smiled at that. Maybe he should get an appointment and find out what he was going to do when he left Wyattville.

His boss expected him back. He'd been okay at hearing that Jake needed a little more time off, but he had made it clear that he wanted Jake back in the saddle. *"You did the only thing you could have,"* he'd said.

Maybe that was true. He'd worked side by side with Marcy for almost eight years. He had trusted her, admired her work ethic and enjoyed her quirky sense of humor. He'd listened to stories about her nieces and nephews and mowed her lawn when she'd sprained her ankle. He'd helped her drag home a Christmas tree and patched a hole in her ceiling when the rain was leaking in. He'd given her dating advice and she'd done the same for him. He'd had at least one beer with her most every Friday night.

There'd never been anything sexual between them. He'd considered her a friend, and if there'd been warning signs, he'd ignored them.

Nobody had any idea that she was part of one of the bigger illegal drug distribution rings in the city—that she'd been on the inside, providing information to the bad guys, making it easy for them to always be one step ahead of the police.

Then, somehow, she'd fallen out of favor. Maybe she'd gotten greedy or maybe her loyalty had been in question. For whatever reason, the bad guys had set her up, had made sure that information was passed on to Jake and others that put her square in the crosshairs.

It could have been an easy bust. She'd had the drugs on her. But she'd decided that she wasn't going to make it easy. Maybe had known that from the beginning it might turn out this way—after all, prison was no place for a cop. Her first shot had killed Officer Howard, her second had damned near killed Jake, had come inches from nicking a major artery and he'd have bled out. But inches mattered, and he'd gotten his own shot off and then it had been over.

But it hadn't really been over. He'd been left to make sense of the whole mess. And maybe he'd accepted this assignment because he'd known that he needed a place to hide out. A place to heal.

And while it wasn't perfect, it wasn't terrible, either. He felt bad about how he'd discounted the assignment initially and the jokes he'd made with his family about how he'd be writing parking tickets and getting stray cats out of trees.

Since arriving in town, he'd busted two teenagers who were shoplifting from Frank Johnson, responded to a domestic disturbance where the estranged husband was violating an order of protection and attended a tricounty gathering of law enforcement to discuss the status of meth production in the region. Tomorrow, he'd be meeting with the bank to discuss security because smaller banks were becoming bigger targets for thieves. Next week, he'd be meeting with the principal of the grade school who had asked him to assist in developing a stranger-awareness program. Evidently an eight-year-old in a neighboring community got approached right before school let out for summer.

It was kind of fun actually. In the city, he'd become pretty specialized—working a lot on drug- and gang-related crime. And for every idiot he put away, five more took his place. The game went on.

He could see how in a smaller community a cop retained his skills because the assignments were all over the map. In fact, when Alice Fenton had come to the station this morning with the look of a woman on a mission, he'd been prepared to take a complaint of some kind. Had already pulled out a blank report in anticipation. When she'd invited him to dinner, he'd been so surprised that he'd said yes without even trying to think up an excuse.

Of course, maybe that had something to do with the fact that she'd mentioned that Tara would also be in attendance. Last night, when Tara had come to the station, calling out Andy's name, her tone almost desperate, he'd thought the worst. And for a brief second had contemplated firing the young man. Then he'd realized the absurdity of that action. First, he was merely the interim chief. He didn't have the authority to make unilateral personnel decisions. And second, how was he going to explain it?

I was jealous of his relationship with a woman who won't give me the time of day.

Yup. That had a nice ring. It was a good thing he

might be giving up police work, because when it got out that he'd lost his mind, nobody would touch him with a ten-foot pole.

When Tara had explained why she needed police assistance, he'd been skeptical. Hell, a monkey would have been skeptical. But she'd been so damn adamant about the door. But then, once they were inside, she'd seemed to readily accept that she'd either imagined the whole thing or somehow been wrong.

Something wasn't right. He'd known her for only a few days, but he'd bet that she didn't have a flighty bone in her body. She was solid. She ran her own business and appeared to be doing a bang-up job. He had stopped in the other restaurant in town and had been unimpressed. The food had been okay, the service fine, but there'd been no warmth, no feeling of inclusion that was ever-present at Nel's. The difference was Tara Thompson.

He hadn't been as intrigued by a woman since... since never. It was just one more thing he hadn't expected to experience in Wyattville. And really rotten timing. What did he have to offer? About as far as he could see into the future was next week.

He'd spoken to Chase this morning. His friend had apologized and said he'd likely be out of town longer than he'd expected. His mother was refusing to do her physical therapy and barely eating. He didn't want to leave her just yet.

Jake had assured him that he was doing fine. Chase had said that he'd spoken to Chief Wilks and the man was recovering. Then he dropped the bombshell that Chief Wilks, who had turned sixty-two the previous year, was talking about retiring. Jake had quickly reminded his good friend that he'd agreed to do this only temporarily, and Chase had confirmed that he understood.

Jake pulled the squad car into his designated parking spot at the municipal building and got out. Frank Johnson and his wife, Ginny, who watched Lori Mae's boys when she was working, were standing next to their car. They'd parked around the side of the building. Riley and Keller stood next to them. Riley held a cake box and Keller had his fist around a wad of balloons. Jake figured it was just seconds before the cake hit the ground and the balloons went airborne.

It was Lori Mae's thirty-fourth birthday and her family intended to surprise her. They'd asked for his help. Lori Mae didn't normally work weekends and he'd had to invent an excuse to get her to come in on a Saturday. He'd told her that he needed help with the stranger-awareness program—had figured that would resonate with her. It had, and when he'd checked in with her just an hour ago, she'd been cruising the internet, identifying resources.

He saw Andy's squad coming down the street

and they waited for him to get parked. Then the group went in, the twins leading the way.

An hour later, he and Lori Mae were the only ones in the station. Cake had been eaten and cleaned up, balloons gushed over, and Frank and Ginny had taken the twins home to wreak havoc on the neighbors. Andy had gone home to catch a nap before his shift started.

Lori Mae had cried. And hugged her boys, her parents, and even Andy and him. Now she was eyeing him. "Pretty tricky," she said.

He smiled. "I thought you might figure it out when you had to work on Saturday."

"No. That sometimes happened when Chief Wilks was here, too. I do think I surprised Alice Fenton though. She wasn't expecting to see me. What did she want?"

"She invited me to dinner."

"I figured as much. We don't have all that many eligible bachelors."

"I think she's married," he said.

"But her daughter's not. She was. Got divorced about a year ago and moved home. Watch out for that one. My husband and I went to school with Madeline. Even though she was a year younger than us, she always sort of scared me. There was something about the look in her eyes. Heck, she scared my husband, who later became a marine with no problem."

"What do you mean?"

"These are just rumors of course, but she supposedly trashed a neighbor's house after they didn't pay her what she thought she deserved for watching their kids. Busted everything up inside and spray-painted the siding. She even let the livestock out of their pens. There were cows all over the county. Police couldn't prove it though because her parents swore that she'd been home the whole night, said they were playing board games. Trust me on this. Even at fifteen, Madeline Fenton wasn't the type to play board games with her parents on a Friday night."

"Well, she's having dinner with her parents on a Saturday night. Mrs. Fenton said that her daughter and Tara Thompson were going to join us."

Lori Mae laughed. "Interesting. I could say something terribly inappropriate about threesomes to my new boss but I suspect Alice just doesn't want to be too obvious. For the last year or so, Madeline's been hot and heavy with Jim Waller, a vice president at the bank. In fact, she started working at the bank shortly after they started dating. I have a few friends who work there. They used to say she spent more time in Jim's office with the door closed than she did at her desk, working. Recently they told me they were pretty sure it had fizzled out. Must be true."

AT 4:00 P.M., TARA WAS on her back underneath the dish machine, swearing like the sailor she'd never been.

The restaurant had been closed for an hour. The company from Minneapolis that she'd hired to replace the window had arrived on schedule, and it had taken them less than fifteen minutes to put the new glass in. She'd been happy to have the ugly plywood removed. Food had been put away and the dining room cleaned, swept and made ready for the next week. But there were still dirty dishes. Everywhere.

They'd managed to keep up for most of the day. However, at one point, toward the end of the lunch hour, a woman, oblivious of the dish crisis, had ordered soup. Tara had smiled, said of course and thought, *Cup your hands, honey, because that's all I got left to put it in.*

Janet had volunteered to tackle the pans and was up to her elbows in suds at the three-compartment sink. Tara had figured she could whip through the other dishes in less than an hour. She hadn't counted on a leaky pipe and a wet floor.

Normally, the commercial dishwasher that Nel had thankfully invested in just two years before Tara had purchased the restaurant ran perfectly. Dishes were loaded into big trays, the trays were gently shoved into the stainless steel wash area, where they were washed and rinsed with very hot water. Each cycle took about ninety seconds.

But today, for some unknown reason, the kitchen gods were messing with her. Every time she washed a load, more water leaked onto the floor and she realized she was going to have a swamp if she didn't get the problem fixed. That's what led her to be on her back, halfway underneath the beast, a flashlight in one hand and a wrench in the other. She had just located the leak and was starting to twist a gasket when she realized that she was no longer alone.

She could see blue jeans. A man's shoes.

She jerked in surprise and hit her forehead on the bottom of the dishwasher.

"Hey, be careful," he said.

Jake Vernelli.

Tara laid her head on the wet floor and closed her eyes. When her heart rate felt something like normal, she resolutely finished tightening the gasket and then awkwardly eased herself out from underneath the machine.

She was flat on her back, looking up at six feet of muscle. He wore casual clothes, dark jeans and a lightweight summer shirt. He was imposing in a uniform but now he looked comfortable, confident, sexy.

"How's the head?" he asked, extending a hand.

She hesitated and then grabbed his hand. His skin was warm and there were calluses on his palm.

With one gentle pull, he helped her get from horizontal back to vertical. "Okay?" he asked.

Not really. She felt light-headed, and it had nothing to do with the bump on her head. Every day she cleared customers' plates and made change for them when they paid their bills. Occasionally, her hand would brush up against another's. But never had it made her weak in the knees. What the hell was wrong with her?

He inclined his head toward the dish machine. "So how's it doing?"

She rolled her eyes. "Not so good." She wiped her hands on her skirt, which was now pretty filthy. "What can I do for you?"

"I understand we're both having dinner with Henry and Alice Fenton. I'd be happy to give you a ride—then you could show me the way."

Janet had stopped washing dishes and was now listening intently. It would seem odd to refuse. Un-neighborly. And in Wyattville, that just wasn't done.

It wasn't as if it was going to be a date. "Did Alice happen to mention that her daughter was also going to be having dinner with us?"

"She did. Is she younger than Bill?"

"Same age. Twins."

She was not going to tell him about Alice's plans to matchmake. She wouldn't betray her friend in that way—and quite frankly, he was probably used to it. Surely well-meaning friends had been pairing him off with potentials for some time. He was employed, polite and had a killer smile to boot.

He was a catch.

That is, for somebody who had their pole in the water. She did not even like the taste of fish and wasn't even sure she remembered how to bait a hook.

Jake scratched his head. "My parents love me but I'm not sure they'd be crazy about me moving back home. It's got to be hard for the Fentons."

"I'm not sure. They don't say much about it." She looked at her watch, then down at her dirty clothes. She still had to meet with Donny. "I probably won't be finished much before dinnertime. I keep an extra set of clothes here, so that's not a problem. Do you want to pick me up a little before seven?"

"What about your van?"

"It'll be fine parked out back."

"Okay. I'll see you then." He left, tossing Janet one of those great smiles on his way out.

FIFTEEN MINUTES BEFORE SEVEN, Jake pulled into the lot behind Nel's. Tara had been watching for him. She pulled the door closed behind her and turned her key in the bolt lock.

She'd cleaned up and changed into a long cotton skirt and a peasant-style blouse, which had flowing sleeves that covered her scars.

She opened the door and slid into the front seat of his car. It was the first time she'd ever been in a Wyattville squad car but certainly not the first time she'd been in a police vehicle. She'd done a ride-along with a couple of different cops when she'd been a reporter.

Jake's vehicle smelled better than the ones in D.C. It smelled like him—sandalwood with a hint of something darker, like amber. There was a metal gate that separated the front seat from the back and a sleek computer screen perched on the dash, both good reminders of how police work was both physical and intellectual.

"How ya doing?" he asked politely, as he pulled out of the lot and headed south.

"Fine," she lied. She was both tired and frustrated. She'd managed to get the leak fixed but Donny had been a no-show. The heat, the extra work, it was all getting to be overwhelming. And it hadn't helped that the phone had rung four times while she'd been plowing her way through the mound of dishes and each time the caller had hung up. It was the sour icing on a really bad cupcake.

She was in a funk. And she was going to have to work really hard to make sure that her bad mood wasn't contagious. She didn't want to ruin anyone else's evening. "It shouldn't be a late night," she said. She tried to put some warmth in her tone. "You know, early to bed, early to rise."

"At least tomorrow isn't a work day for either of us. Nel's is closed on Sunday, right?"

"Yes. You have the day off, too, right?"

"Yes. Chase or Chief Wilks or whoever did it was smart to get an agreement with the county police that they'll provide coverage on Sunday as well as dispatch during the evenings and nights. It allows a small department to keep labor expenses somewhat under control. By the way, I forgot to mention that your window looks good."

"Yes. It's nice to have the place looking like it should."

They were quiet the rest of the way, Tara only speaking to give Jake the necessary directions. They pulled into the Fentons' long lane and came to rest in front of the handsome two-story farm-house.

When she opened her car door, Tara could smell the pot roast. It would be delicious. There was no doubt about that.

Henry met them on the front porch. "About time you got here," he muttered, looking at Tara. "Alice wanted to send out a search party. Didn't want your roast beef to get too done. Woman never worries about *my* roast beef."

Tara wrinkled her nose at her landlord. "Shush now," she said. "Henry, this is Jake Vernelli. Jake, my landlord, Henry Fenton, who is not normally so cranky."

Henry grinned broadly, showing his yellowed, crooked teeth. "I haven't forgotten your loose tile. I'll get over soon."

"I'm not worried," Tara said. She turned to Jake. "The Fentons are the best landlords in Minnesota."

Jake stuck his hand out. "Pleasure, sir. Thanks for the dinner invitation."

Alice, dusting her hands on her worn apron, came out to the porch. "What are you all doing out here talking? My gravy is getting thicker by the minute."

"And you thought I was cranky?" Henry teased, his arm around Tara's shoulder.

Alice ignored him and ushered them toward the dining room. "We're certainly grateful that you were available to fill in for our chief. I hope you're getting settled, Jake."

Madeline, wearing very tight white pants and a low-cut green shirt that emphasized her green eyes, stood next to the table. She had a pitcher of water in her hand and was filling glasses.

Alice made a sweeping gesture, as if she were showing off a new car. "Jake, this is my daughter, Madeline. She works at the bank. Head teller. Madeline, Jake Vernelli, our new police chief."

"Just interim," Jake corrected. He extended his arm to shake Madeline's hand.

"I understand you're from Minneapolis," Madeline said. "You must be dying of boredom here.

We're going to have to find some fun for you." Her voice was low, almost raspy. She looked at Tara. "Hello," she said.

"Hi, Madeline. How's it going?" Tara asked, trying to be nice.

Madeline looked at Jake. "Better now."

Tara snuck a look at Alice and Henry to see if they were embarrassed by their daughter's actions but neither seemed to notice. She figured it had been going on for so long that they were immune. Or perhaps just hopeful that something, or someone, would get her out of their house.

"Please, sit down," Alice said. She motioned for Tara to take the chair opposite of Jake. Madeline slid onto the chair next to him.

Jake accepted the platter of roast beef that Alice passed his way. He took a slice and passed it to Madeline. When she accepted the dish, her fingers caressed Jake's strong hands. He didn't react.

Oh, good grief, thought Tara. She looked around the table, desperately trying to focus on something besides Madeline making a fool of herself. Her gaze settled on Henry. His leathery skin was sunburned and his nose was peeling. "Henry, you look as if you've spent some time in the sun."

"Well, I sure as hell haven't been going to one of those tanning salons." He looked at his wife. "Alice wants a shed for all her quilting and sewing supplies. Problem is the man I hired to help me fell off a ladder and hurt his back. I've been doing the best I can."

Jake looked up from his plate. He directed his attention to Alice. "I think I may have died and gone to heaven. This is delicious." Then he shifted his attention to Henry. "I put myself through college working construction. Maybe I could help you."

The roast beef suddenly tasted like glue. Alice had always been the matchmaker, so Tara was confident that Henry's comments had been innocent and that he wasn't looking for a way to push Madeline and Jake together. However, was Jake looking for a reason to spend more time with the Fentons? Was he attracted to Madeline?

"Why Jake," Alice practically cooed. Clearly her plan was working even better than she'd dared to hope. "That's so nice of you. We promise not to take up too much time."

Jake smiled at her. "I'd be glad to help."

She turned toward Tara. "So tell us about the picnic."

Tara was happy enough to do that—at least she could focus on Alice and Henry and ignore Jake and Madeline, whose breasts were about to jump out of her shirt. Tara told them about the parade and the dunk tank and even the sack races. Of course, she left out the part where she and Jake had become tangled. She didn't want to give Madeline the impression that she was competition. The woman might really get angry, puff out her chest even more, and there would be a wardrobe malfunction of great magnitude.

They were almost finished when Tara asked about Bill. She felt it would be rude not to.

"Oh, he's fine. Just fine. He's getting married, you know."

She did know. Alice had told her at least five times. "Did you get a chance to meet his fiancée?"

"Oh, yes. She's a lovely girl. So smart. Has a good job."

"Did Bill find a job yet?"

Alice looked at Henry. He was staring down at his empty dinner plate.

"Why, he's in business," she said. "Sales. Same as before."

Madeline leaned forward in her chair. "Yes, Mother. What is it exactly that darling Bill does?"

Alice pushed back her chair and briskly started clearing the table. The atmosphere was acutely charged. Madeline got up and threw her napkin on the table. "I've got a prior engagement," she said. She braced her arms on the table and leaned toward Jake, and like a good banker, gave him an even better look at her assets. "Maybe another time?" she said, her tone suggestive. Then she left the room without a word to her mother, father or Tara.

Alice stacked dishes with sharp, almost jerky movements. Henry shrugged, looking uncomfortable. Tara wanted to say something to make them feel better, to make the situation less awkward, but she was speechless. It was one thing for Madeline to be rude to her but quite another for her to snub her own parents in the presence of guests. That was something a thirteen-year-old pulled, not a grown woman.

The moment passed when Alice delivered big pieces of peach pie with vanilla ice cream along with cups of steaming coffee. They ate their dessert and made small talk. They stayed another twenty minutes before Jake pushed his own chair back.

They said their goodbyes and went back outside. Tara looked off to the west, where the sky was starting to darken with lovely shades of purple and streaks of red. It was still very warm.

Jake unlocked his squad car and opened the door for Tara. She hadn't expected that and stumbled over her thank-you. "It's good there's a breeze," she added hastily, aware that Alice stood on the porch and could likely hear their conversation.

Jake didn't answer. He started the car. She rolled down her window. "Don't forget that you need to drop me off at Nel's. My car is there," she said, more loudly than normal.

He looked at her, one eyebrow raised. "Okay." He put the car in Reverse, made a quick turn, and they were on their way. Tara took a quick look over her shoulder and saw that Alice was still standing on the porch. Watching.

"Is there a reason you're yelling?" he asked.

"I wasn't really yelling." She took two deep yoga-style breaths. "It's just that I don't want Alice thinking the wrong thing."

"Which is?"

She resisted the urge to sigh. He was deliberately pushing her buttons and she was too tired to do the dance. "She obviously is hoping that you'll have some interest in Madeline. Alice is not just my landlord, she's my friend, too. I do not want her to think that there's something between the two of us."

She waited for him to respond but he didn't seem inclined. Nervous with the silence, she plunged ahead. "Look, this is a ridiculous conversation. Let's talk about something else."

He didn't say anything for a minute, then he smiled and pressed a hand to his firm, flat stomach. "I've always heard about roast beef that melted in your mouth but I've never actually experienced it until tonight."

"Thank you," she whispered. "And, yes, Alice is a wonderful cook," she added in her normal voice.

"I got the impression that Madeline and her twin brother aren't close."

Tara looked out the side window. "I'm not sure what happened. Bill rarely talked about Madeline but when he did, it was pretty apparent that there was a whole lot of resentment. I don't know about what. He never said."

"Families. Hard to figure out sometimes."

"True. It was nice of you to volunteer to help Henry with the shed," she said. "I didn't realize that you had those skills."

"I get by. Good enough for shed building anyway. I like working with my hands. My dad is an amateur carpenter, and I've helped him on several projects."

Now she understood the calluses on his palms. She'd shared a love of words with her dad. He'd been a newspaper editor and she'd been proud to follow somewhat in his footsteps. She'd expected to have lots of time to learn from him. Then life had taken a very unexpected turn when her parents, coming home from a social event, had both been killed in an automobile accident, victims of a drunk driver. The shock had paralyzed Tara. She'd somehow managed to arrange their funerals. Two months later, she'd met Michael. Now, in retrospect, she wondered if her judgment had been impaired.

"Well, hopefully, the two of you can make a dent in it during the six weeks that you're here."

He kept his eyes on the road. "If it takes a couple extra weeks, I don't think Chase will mind me staying at his place."

What kind of arrangement had he made with his current employer? "You must have had a lot of vacation time built up in order to take that much time off."

She didn't think he was going to answer the question. Or move at all. They were stopped at the first intersection past the Fentons. There was no reason he couldn't go. There wasn't another car on the road.

"Jake," she prompted.

He turned to look at her. "I'm on a leave of absence. I got shot in the leg about three months ago."

Shot. He'd been hurt. Her dessert rumbled in her stomach. "I had no idea. I mean, no one could tell. You're not limping or anything."

He smiled. "I paid attention to what the physical therapist told me to do."

"Did they catch the man who did it?"

"Woman. She was my partner. I returned fire and killed her."

His partner. The cops she'd known in D.C. were closer to their partners than to their sisters and brothers. It was a tight bond. "That must have been horrible," she said. She reached out and touched his arm. "What happened?"

Jake stared at her hand, then slowly lifted his eyes until they were staring at each other. "I don't talk about it much."

It was the same thing he'd said about his divorce. "I…I'm just so sorry that happened to you. You must have trusted her a great deal. And it would have felt like such a betrayal, like a piece of you had turned bad."

He tilted his head ever so slightly and seemed to consider her words. "You know," he said finally, "you're the first person to say it exactly that way. How did you know?"

She knew a lot about trusting the wrong person. About the bone-deep pain of being connected to someone and being terribly wrong about that person. "I…" Could she tell him? Could she take the chance? She just didn't know. "I'm not sure," she lied.

He shoved the car into Park and leaned across the seat. "Tara," he said, very quietly. Then he cupped the sides of her face with his palms, and kissed her.

Gentle at first. His lips were warm and soft, and she could taste coffee and peaches. It had been so long and it felt so good. She opened her mouth, and he didn't hesitate. The kiss went deep, his tongue in her mouth, consuming, possessing, owning. And just when she thought it would end, it didn't.

When he finally pulled back, he was breathing hard.

Yikes. The man's mouth is a weapon. He should carry a permit.

"I've been wanting to do that since the first night I met you. And if it matters," he added, a smile in his brown eyes, "you're the first girl I ever kissed on a gravel road in the middle of nowhere."

The absurdity of the situation hit her. They were parking, or rather in Park, in a police car, and necking like high school kids. What the hell had Alice put in that peach pie? "I'm not looking for a relationship," she said.

"And I'm only here for a few more weeks."

It was the perfect arrangement. No strings. "That's fair," she whispered.

He ran his thumb across her bottom lip. "At the risk of moving way too fast and you jumping out of this car, I've just got to ask—when we get to town, will you come to Chase's house?"

They both knew what the real question was. And she desperately wanted to say yes. For one night to forget that he was something she couldn't have. To forget that she'd made choices that couldn't be undone. To be young again.

"My house is closer," she whispered. She pointed to the right. "Turn that way."

He didn't need to be told twice. He turned and accelerated. When they crested the next hill, they saw the smoke.

"Oh, my God. My house is on fire," she said, just as the squad car's radio crackled to life.

Chapter Eight

He and Tara arrived from one direction at almost the exact same moment that Wyattville's volunteer firefighters arrived from another. It was the garage, not the house, that was burning.

"Stay back," he ordered and jumped from the car. The breeze Tara had celebrated earlier wasn't helping them now. The garage was fully engulfed in flames and the house would go next.

Unless they could work very quickly. He watched the men scramble down from the truck and efficiently move to get hoses connected. While this was a volunteer unit, Jake could immediately sense that they knew what the hell they were doing. He was grateful. Tara did not deserve to lose her home.

Once the water was pouring on the flames, he turned to find her. He had a moment of panic when she wasn't standing by his squad car. Then he saw her, standing next to Alice, who had arrived along with a steady stream of what must be other neighbors. The older woman had her arm around Tara's shoulder, but Tara wasn't hiding her eyes, hoping that it would all go away. She was scanning the crowd, looking.

She was expecting to see someone. Who, damn it?

It took thirty minutes to extinguish the fire. Once the ruins were simply smoldering, the fire chief made his way toward Jake. "Evening, sir," he said. "I'm Chad Wilson. Toby is my dad. He said he's been doing some repairs for you."

Jake shook the firefighter's hand. "What do you think, Chad?"

"I think we're damn lucky that her van wasn't parked inside with a full tank of gas. It would have made it tough to handle in this wind. The building is a total loss."

"Is there an arson investigator in this community?"

Chad nodded. "I'm a trained investigator. We've got some additional resources we can call in Minneapolis if we need to. However, this one isn't that tough. There's no question that this fire was deliberately set."

"How do you know that?"

Jake whirled around. He hadn't seen Tara approaching. Her face was pale, her skirt was dirty from the blowing soot, but she didn't look surprised to hear that it had been arson.

"Hey, Tara. Sorry about the garage. But at least we saved the house."

"Thank you, Chad. I'm grateful. Really. Can you tell me how you know it was arson?"

Chad looked uncomfortable. "I really shouldn't be saying much more, Tara. Not until...that is... until you've made a statement."

Oh, boy, he thought. Her face colored red with frustration or anger or a mixture of both. "A statement," she said between clenched teeth. "*I* have to make a statement."

Now Chad was looking at the ground. "Chief Vernelli here should take your statement. Make sure your whereabouts in the last hour are accounted for. Hell, Tara, I'm doing this for your protection."

"I did not burn my own garage down," Tara said. "That's the most ridiculous thing I've ever heard. And if you had any sense..." She started to point her finger in Chad's face.

Jake decided to save the man. After all, he and the other firefighters had saved the house. "I don't need to get a statement from Tara. I know where she was for the last hour. With me."

That got Chad to raise his head. And his eyes were full of interest.

Jake held up a hand. "We were dinner guests at the Fentons'." His tone said it all: *Stop your spec-*

ulation. This part of the discussion is over. "Now why do you think the fire was deliberately set?"

"Multiple points of origin, and somebody cut a damn hole in the roof to make it spread faster."

"I want to take a look," Jake said. Maybe there would be something that would lead him to the arsonist's identity.

"We've got to wait for it to cool down. Tomorrow morning, when it's daylight, I'll be back. If there's anything in there that will help us identify who set the fire, you'll be the first to know. Right now, though, I'm going to secure the area with some crime scene tape." Chad turned toward Tara. "A couple of my men will stick around for a few hours. Sometimes there can be ash hot enough to reignite, and with this wind you might be in danger in the house."

"She's not going to be in the house."

Now Tara turned on him. "If you think..." She stopped. "Chad, will you excuse us?" she asked.

He looked very disappointed. "Sure."

Just as soon as the man was far enough away that their conversation could be private, Jake jumped in. "Tara, I'm just the temporary guy who maybe doesn't know anything. But something is not right. You've had nothing but trouble for the last few days. Now, we're dealing with someone who is crazy enough to deliberately start a fire on a windy summer evening. You're in danger. You need to tell me what's going on or I'm not going to be able to help you."

He could see the indecision in her eyes and for a brief second, he thought he'd gotten through. Then she squared her shoulders. "I understand that it's probably not in my best interest to stay here tonight. But I do need to get some things from my house. Then I'll see if I can stay with Alice and Henry for the night."

"Stay with me," he said. He lowered his voice even more. "I'm not expecting anything. I mean, what happened in the car was pretty damn nice. And I'm not going to lie and say that I didn't really appreciate the invitation to come back here with you. But after this, well, I know you've got other things on your mind. I just want you to be safe."

"But…"

He went for the final blow. "If Chad is right and the fire was deliberately set, somebody is at best trying to irritate you, or at worst trying to hurt you. You might be putting Alice and Henry in danger if it becomes known that you're staying there."

She chewed on her lip. It made him remember how sweet she tasted. He looked away. Tara was going to sleep in one bedroom and he was going to sleep in another. Only a jerk would think he could pick up where he'd left off after something like this.

Tara looked him in the eye. "I don't want anybody to be in danger because of me. Anybody."

He got the strangest sense that she was warning him. Of what? "I'm a cop, Tara. I can take care of myself. I can take care of you."

She didn't respond. Just turned and went inside her house. Jake walked over to where Andy was shooting the breeze with a couple of the firefighters. "Hey, Chief," the young man said. "Got lucky here tonight, didn't we?"

He'd almost gotten lucky. Real lucky.

Damn, he was as bad as Chad Wilson. He gave himself a mental head slap. He needed to get his mind out of the gutter and get it back in the game.

In this weather, this could have been a catastrophe. Even though the rain had been fast and furious that first night he'd arrived in Wyattville, the consistent heat over the past few weeks and the wind the past couple of days had taken a toll. The fire could not only have spread to the house, it was possible that it might have spread to the dry grass across the road and just kept on burning. Wildfires didn't just happen out West.

It wouldn't have been the easiest call to make. *Hey, Chase. Your town, yeah the one you gave me to watch over, is nothing but smoke and ashes.*

Whoever had done this was either really stupid or really crazy. "Who called it in, Andy?"

"Some guy. Didn't give his name. No caller ID."

Even though it was eighty degrees, a chill ran down Jake's spine. Somebody had deliberately set a fire and then called it in. Had he or she wanted Tara to be there, wanted to watch her reaction, her despair?

Jake scanned the crowd. For the first time, he hated being an outsider. Most everyone was a stranger to him. He didn't know their faces, their habits, their quirks. "Andy, take a look around. Is there anybody here that you don't know?"

He waited while the young man scanned the crowd. "Nope. A couple people that I haven't seen for a few months, but everybody belongs."

Jake didn't feel any better. Was it possible that someone Tara trusted was trying to hurt her?

"I'm going to call the county and see if they can loan us somebody to watch this property tonight."

"I could stay here," Andy volunteered.

"I want you to go find Donny Miso. If he doesn't have a really good alibi for tonight, you call me."

TARA WAS QUIET on the way into town. He figured she was probably exhausted. It was almost eleven and Jake knew that she'd probably been up at around five that morning. When he parked his squad car in front of Chase's brick ranch and killed the engine, she just sat there.

"Planning on coming in?" he asked.

"Life is funny, you know," she said.

"'Funny ha-ha' or 'funny, this cannot be happening'?"

"Tonight, mostly the latter. If you'd have told me this morning that I was going to end up spending the night sleeping in Chase Montgomery's house, I'd have thought you were crazy. But here I am."

Yeah, life was funny. He'd been a decorated police officer, one of the first of his class to make detective. It was going to be his life's work. Now look at him. Would his life ever be the same? "I guess," he said, "the trick is to roll with the punches, go with the flow, make lemonade from lemons. Pick your cliché."

"Know when to hold 'em, know when to fold 'em," she said.

She sounded weary. Since the first moment he'd met her, she'd seemed to have tireless energy and such a great sense of purpose. Nel's was more than just a restaurant to her. It was a place where people gathered, where stories were told, where friendships were cemented. It was her contribution back to a community that she loved.

He absolutely hated seeing her so defeated. "It's going to be okay, Tara. Tomorrow is a new day. You'll be more rested and ready to take it on. And we'll catch the person who did this."

She drew in a deep breath. "A garage is nothing. I know that. I didn't even keep anything of value in there." Her voice cracked at the end. He could hear the tears that she was trying so desperately to hold back. That was his undoing.

"Oh, Tara," he said, pulling her into his arms. He rubbed her back.

She pressed her face against his shoulder and started to cry as if her heart was breaking. Big choking sobs. Tears that wet his shirt.

He held her, feeling clumsy and inept and more angry than ever. She was hurting and somebody was going to pay. "It's going to be okay. I promise, Tara. I promise."

TARA WAS MORTIFIED that she'd cried all over Jake's shirt. He'd just been so nice. And it continued after they got inside. He showed her the empty bedroom and the bath. He got her a glass of water and offered her magazines to read. When she declined, he turned on the television and asked her if she had a favorite program. Then he offered her a bowl of ice cream.

Finally, exhausted from his politeness, she took a shower. She knew she reeked of smoke and did not want to leave the smell in Chase's house. There was expensive shampoo in the guest shower, and it made her wonder if solemn Chase had an occasion to entertain female guests who enjoyed the little luxuries of life. She rinsed and rinsed and wished she could wash away the day.

She finally shut off the water, got out, dried off and put on clean underwear and a big T-shirt that she'd stuffed in her overnight bag. Finally, she brushed her teeth. She turned off the lights, slipped into the strange bed and stared into the darkness. Then she got out of bed, shuffled her way to the door and locked it.

Was she locking Jake out or herself in? He'd been a gentleman tonight. After all, she *had* invited him to her place. Neither of them were kids. They both knew the score. Classic hookup.

Except that she'd never really been a hookup kind of girl. She'd dated a lot in college and had two relationships that each lasted more than a year. She'd slept with both of those men and had mourned the loss of the closeness when each relationship had ended. Then there'd been Michael. He'd told her that she was the best thing that had ever happened to him. She'd liked believing that. She'd been ready to settle down.

Tonight when Jake had held her face in his hands and kissed her, she'd felt terribly unsettled. But in a wonderful way. The need had been almost more than she could bear. She had wanted him with a ferociousness that bordered on scary. She'd suggested her house because, quite frankly, she wasn't sure she could last until they got to town. And he'd been pretty much keeping pace.

At her house, he'd kept his professional distance. No one would have known that just minutes before, they'd been devouring each other or that they'd had plans to heat up the sheets. And then he'd literally held her at arm's length until she'd thrown herself at him and cried all over his shirt.

Had it been that easy for him to forget about the kiss? Or what almost came next? She didn't think she would ever forget it.

That, she decided as she crawled back into bed, was the reason she locked the door.

Once in bed, in the quiet darkness, she allowed herself to think about what she'd been avoiding since she'd seen the flames dancing out of her garage. Should she run now, without knowing for sure if it was Michael? What if it wasn't? She'd be giving up everything she'd worked for. What if it was him? Could she afford to wait even another day? Her mind was whirling. She forced herself to breathe deep, to calm herself. She closed her eyes and envisioned spring flowers, miles and miles of them. She thought of puppies and snowflakes and warm cherry pie.

She thought of nothing, hoping desperately that her brain would shut down.

But it didn't. When sleep finally came, her dreams were wild and angry. Michael had found her. He waited for her. Just like before. She opened the front door of her house and he stood in the kitchen. "I'll never let you go," he ranted.

Tara lunged toward the door but he stopped her. He grabbed her, his arms as strong as a vise, and she knew that fighting back was useless. He twisted her arm and the pain flamed. She looked down. Her arm hung at her side, flopping like a wet noodle. Michael laughed, holding his arms high above his head. In Michael's hand, he held a long thin bone, covered with blood. Her bone, her blood. She looked down again at the flaccid flesh at her side and screamed in horror.

"Tara, Tara," he called to her.

She couldn't move. Blood poured out of her arm, pooling around her feet. He was going to make good on his promise—this time he was going to kill her.

"Somebody help me," she screamed.

She woke up when the bedroom door flew open and slammed against the wall. It hung off its hinges and Jake filled the doorway. His hair was sticking up, his eyes looked huge, and he had his gun pointed at her.

"I'm okay," she managed, grateful that he'd turned the hallway light on. Not only did she hate waking up in the dark but she didn't want him shooting her by mistake. "I had a bad dream."

She heard him sigh. "Tara. You scared ten years off me." He came close enough that his knees brushed up against the bed. His chest was moving as he sucked in air. "Do you want to talk about it?" he asked finally.

"No," she replied honestly, not even able to look at him. Had she screamed out Michael's name? Had she been that careless? She was terribly afraid that the tears that threatened would fall any minute. Jake had been through that once already tonight. He certainly didn't deserve another round.

"Tara, that was some dream."

She hadn't had that particular nightmare for months. Had thought she had finally left it behind. "Yeah. Maybe I should have had that ice cream," she said, hoping like heck that he'd let it go. She yawned and made a big production out of covering her mouth.

He got the message and stepped back.

And as crazy as it seemed, even though she was covered with a blanket and a sheet, she felt suddenly cold. "Jake," she said. She could explain. Really should. But then he'd look at her with the same disgusted look that the cops in D.C. had. She couldn't bear that. She never wanted to see that look in anyone's eyes again. And then he'd have all kinds of questions. Questions that she couldn't answer.

"Yeah?" he prompted, his tone patient.

"Nothing," she said.

He stood there, motionless. The only sound in the quiet night was his breathing. After a minute, he turned and left, doing his best to close her bedroom door behind him.

Once he was gone, she felt cold and very alone. Perhaps more so than ever, because for those few minutes when his male scent had filled her room and his quiet competence had helped steady her, she'd almost been able to forget that he wanted a woman who wouldn't lie to him.

Chapter Nine

The next morning, shortly after the sun rose past the horizon, Jake rolled down the windows of his squad car and drove to Tara's house. Before leaving, he'd made sure she was still sleeping. He had stood in the wrecked doorway of her room and watched her for several minutes. Her face had been relaxed, her dreams peaceful.

They hadn't been peaceful the night before. Had scared the hell out of him. It had been one really bizarre night. Full of highs and lows and every kind of emotion. Euphoria when she'd invited him back to her house. Outrage when he'd seen the fire. Sadness when she'd collapsed in his arms and cried her heart out. Awkwardness when they'd come inside. He'd been the host and she'd been the quiet guest who didn't want to cause any trouble.

Then she'd taken a very long shower. Not that he'd been timing her or listening or hell no, envisioning her naked in there. He'd heard the bed squeak and that had caused him a few uncomfortable moments. Flipping through the television channels, he'd finally landed on an old Adam Sandler movie.

The next thing he knew, her screams had awakened him from a sound sleep. For just a brief moment, he'd been back in a dark warehouse, and Marcy had been pointing a gun at his heart. And the screaming had been in his head.

Then he'd realized where he was and had run for her room, sure that someone had somehow managed to get inside. And the damn door had been locked. He'd have to get that fixed before Chase returned.

When he'd found her safe, he'd wanted to hold her. And not let go until both of them stopped shaking. But then she'd played the It's Nothing card. *It's nothing* you need to worry about. *It's nothing* that we're going to discuss. That's what had kept him up for the rest of the night. That and the fact that every time he closed his eyes, he saw her sitting up in bed, her ridiculously long-sleeved big T-shirt slipping off her shoulder, showing soft, silky skin.

About four, he'd stopped pretending that going back to sleep was an option. He'd showered—yes, a cold one—and that had helped some. Then he'd watched some early-morning news programs and when it was light, had decided to stop screwing around. Before leaving he'd written Tara a note, telling her that he might be gone for several hours—

that he was going to check on her garage and then go to the office to finish up some paperwork.

He didn't see another car on the road until he pulled into Tara's lane and realized that Chad Wilson was already working the scene. Chad glanced up as he got out of the car.

"I'm about done here, Chief." He pointed to a blue evidence bag. "Got everything I need."

"Find anything?"

"Confirmation of what I thought yesterday. Three points of origin. No obvious accelerant, which tells me the guy was either really confident or lucky—maybe both."

"What do you mean?"

"He had to light one spot, move to the second and finally the third. By the time that third one got lit, there was probably a fair amount of smoke. He still had to get out. Which he did, because there's no dead body inside. Which I'm grateful for. It would have really cranked up the paperwork."

Jake smiled. True but it might have allowed him to get a decent night's sleep. "Anything else?"

"No. But if I had to hazard a guess, it's probably not the guy's first fire. Not a pro but some technique." Chad peeled off his gloves and the booties covering his shoes. "I'll do the official report, get a copy to you, and another one for Tara's insurance company." He opened his car door and shoved his bag inside. "Hey, Chief. I understand from my dad that your truck is ready. You can pick it up anytime."

"Great. I'm going to put a couple hours in at the office, then I'll run by and get it." Jake got in his car, started it and dialed Andy's cell phone number. The man answered on the third ring, sounding sleepy.

"Andy, it's Chief Vernelli. Did you talk to Donny Miso last night?"

"Uh…yeah. Let me get my notes."

Jake started driving toward the police station. Saw just one car on the road. As it went past, the driver waved. Just being friendly.

Except that not everybody was friendly in Wyattville. Somebody was being very unfriendly to Tara. And he couldn't shake the feeling that she knew more than she was telling.

"Okay, Chief. I found him at the Double-Pull. Bartender confirmed that he'd gotten there around eight."

"What was he doing before that?"

"Said he was sitting in Washington Park, on a bench."

"Can anybody confirm that?"

"He said there were some kids on skateboards, doing jumps off the ramps. He thought they'd probably remember him. I tried to find them at the park but they'd gone home. I'll swing by today. Oh, by the way, Janet called. She didn't have your number. She said it was important that she talk to you."

"To me? Not to Tara?"

"Definitely you, Chief."

Jake took down Janet's number, thanked Andy and concluded the call. He dialed Janet's number. She answered on the first ring.

"Hi, Janet. It's Jake Vernelli. Andy said that you wanted to talk to me."

"How's Tara?"

"Okay, I think."

"Good. Look, I've got something to tell you. It might not be anything but when I heard about the fire, I knew I had to say something. This isn't the first fire that got deliberately set in Wyattville."

Jake thought it was odd that Chad Wilson hadn't said anything about other fires. "When were the others?"

"Almost seventeen years ago. My son was sixteen. The same age as Bill Fenton. They were best friends. Inseparable. It was the summer before their junior year."

That explained why Chad hadn't said anything. He doubted there could be any connection, but given that Janet wasn't known for gossiping or even talking unnecessarily, he didn't want to shut her down. "Tell me about the fires."

"A couple barns were burned down. Some livestock was killed. That made a lot of people angry."

"What happened?"

"My son was arrested. He never went to jail or anything. We got a lawyer and, ultimately, the charges were dropped because there wasn't any evidence. But some people never did believe he was innocent and it was difficult for him. I knew he didn't do it. He wasn't that kind of kid."

"Who started the fires, Janet?"

"I don't know for sure. But I always thought that Bill Fenton had something to do with it, because the two of them stopped being friends and they never spoke again after that summer. I asked my son but he would never say. I guess he figured he didn't want anybody else to suffer the kind of public condemnation that he'd been subjected to."

"And you think this has something to do with the fire at Tara's house?"

"I don't know. All I know is that I don't want it to start up again. That's all I got to say. Goodbye." She hung up.

Jake drummed his fingers on the steering wheel, not sure what to think of the conversation. It seemed pretty far-fetched that Bill Fenton had come back and burned down Tara's garage when he was supposedly moving on with his life. Hell, the man was getting married. But there was the odd exchange between Madeline and her mother, and now that he thought about it, Henry's behavior had seemed a bit off, too.

He might just do a little checking on the man, just to be sure the Fentons had a good read on their son. He pulled up outside the police station, but instead of getting out he started to think of all the things that he'd rather do on a bright, beautiful Sunday morning. Nobody was expecting him, it was his day off. And, as silly as it sounded, he was anxious to drive Veronica again.

It was a long shot that Toby Wilson would be at work, but Jake took the chance. He made a quick right and then a left and pulled up to the two-bay garage. One overhead door was open, and he could see Toby with his head stuck under the hood of a black SUV.

In a matter of minutes, Jake had walked around Veronica, dutifully admired the work, paid the bill and pocketed the keys. "I'll be back in just a few minutes, Toby. I'm going to drop the squad car off at the station and then walk back to get my truck."

It took less than ten minutes to get it done. As he pulled away from the garage, he waved to Toby, happy to be in his truck once again. As he cruised down the street, he thought about picking up some pastries and coffee—Andy had shared that the grocery store had a decent bakery. And Tara seemed to really like the sweet stuff. Maybe they could eat outside on Chase's patio and read the paper.

On the way through Wyattville, he glanced at Nel's. The front windows all looked secure. On a whim, he decided to check the back door. When he turned into the lot, his thoughts started to race. Not because of what he saw but rather, because of what he didn't see.

Tara's vehicle wasn't there. Had someone stolen the old van? Jake got out of his car and started to run up the wooden steps to Nicholi's apartment, thinking the man might have seen something. At the last minute he realized that he was going to scare the hell out of Nicholi if he didn't calm down. The man would think it was about Andy and he'd assume the worst.

When Nicholi opened the door, Jake was casually leaning against the railing. "Hey, Nicholi. How's it going?"

"Pretty good. My apartment is hot already, though. Doesn't seem as if the old air conditioner can keep up."

Maybe that was why he was sweating, Jake thought. Right.

"Last night I thought Tara left her van here. I was surprised that I didn't see it in the lot."

"She came by about ten minutes ago and got it. Didn't get a chance to talk to her. She waved but seemed as if she might be in a hurry. Darn girl is always doing something."

Yes, but what. And why? "Okay, thanks, Nicholi. Keep cool." Jake returned to his truck and started toward Tara's house. He was a half a mile away when he saw what appeared to be Tara's van in the far distance.

She was leaving town. He sped up and got close. Not too close that she could see him tailing her but close enough that she couldn't lose him.

She turned south and he followed her onto the two-lane highway. Finally she merged onto the interstate, heading toward the Twin Cities. Jake gripped the steering wheel tighter. What the hell was she doing and where the hell was she going? What could be so important that she had to take care of it instead of returning to her home? Surely she had to be curious about what Chad Wilson was going to say about the fire?

Jake understood the fear that settled in his chest, threatening to take his breath away. He'd been almost able to convince himself to dismiss the wariness he'd seen in her eyes. That he'd imagined she was hiding something. Now, with this unexpected trip to the city, she forced him to admit that she might have secrets that he couldn't ignore.

Seventy minutes later Tara turned her van into a downtown Minneapolis parking lot. He barely kept himself from jumping from the truck, running up to her and shaking the truth out of her. Instead he parked the old truck a couple of rows back and to the left. He watched her cross the street and walk up the steps to the Public Library.

She kept her head down, not making eye contact

with anyone. She moved so quickly that he almost lost her when she suddenly stepped into one of the elevators. He waited just long enough to see that it stopped at the third floor before he caught the next one. In less than a minute after reaching the third floor, he found her, already seated at a computer terminal, her left side toward him. He backed up, putting some distance between the two of them. He grabbed a newspaper, found a table, angled his chair so that he could see her and pretended to read.

He couldn't see what she stared at. But she never even glanced around, just kept her eyes fixed on the screen. The only thing that moved was her wrist as she directed the mouse. There were people coming and going but nobody approached her or tried to make contact. The librarian at the front counter ignored her.

An hour later, Jake didn't know anything new. Tara hadn't even shifted in her chair. He was just about to move closer when she suddenly pushed herself away from the computer, stopping as quickly as she'd started. He pulled the paper up in front of his face, peering just over the top. She waited for the elevator, looking neither to her left or her right, just at the floor. Within a minute, the doors opened and she disappeared from sight.

Jake threw the newspaper on the table and headed for the stairs. He reached the lobby just in time to see Tara push through the turnstile at the front door. He raced after her, barely keeping his temper under control. He watched her eat up the sidewalk, her long strides even and efficient. He followed at only a slightly slower pace.

An hour later, he watched the van turn into the lot behind the restaurant. Tara had come straight back with the exception of a brief stop at the McDonald's on the outskirts of Minneapolis.

He waited ten minutes before pulling into the lot and parking next to her. He knocked on the back door. She opened it and motioned him in.

"Good morning," she said. "Did you get your paperwork done?"

"Yeah. What's going on here?" He made his inquiry casual.

She made a sweeping motion toward the butcher-block table that was covered with carrots, celery and potatoes. "I like to prep on Sunday for Monday. I'll cut up these vegetables, put them in five-gallon buckets and cover them with water. Really helps expedite the soup-making process."

He did not give a damn about soup. "I figured you might sleep in."

"I did for a while. Then I came here."

She was lying. And not missing a beat. Damn it. Damn her. He fought to keep his tone neutral. "I thought you might be interested in what Chad Wilson had to say?"

"I called him shortly after the two of you spoke. He said you'd just left to go to the station."

Which made her think that he'd be tied up for a few hours. Maybe she'd even driven by and verified that his squad car was there. She would have been confident that she had plenty of time to make a quick trip to the city. To the library.

It wasn't even noon and he badly needed a drink.

"Did he tell you what he'd found?" he asked.

"Yes. Seems as if it wasn't much more than he knew last night."

"What did you think he would find?" Jake asked.

She shrugged. "I had no idea. I guess I hoped he'd find some way to identify the person who did this."

"And you don't have any idea?"

She stared at his hand and he realized that he'd been drumming his fingers on the table. She drove him crazy. He'd interrogated murderers and never let them see him sweat. She turned him into a fresh-out-of-the-academy grunt who was about to beg. *Please, please, tell me the truth.*

"I have no idea."

He didn't believe her. She was proving to be a very good liar. She was hiding something and damn it, if it was the last thing he did, he was going to figure it out. He wasn't going to be stupid this time—he wasn't going to let his personal feelings get in the way of good judgment. He wasn't going to fail himself or others again.

"Well, I guess I'll shove off," he said. He needed to pound something. Hard. Maybe Henry would want to work on the shed. Then he could beat the hell out of some unsuspecting lumber.

She gave a small wave with her hand and started peeling carrots as if it was her life's ambition.

Chapter Ten

Five days later, on Friday morning, it was so hot that even hardened coffee drinkers had turned to iced tea. Tara set a glass down in front of one of her lunch regulars, laughing when the glass, wet with humidity, almost slipped out of her hand.

"Sorry about that," she offered. "You were almost wearing this."

"No problem. It might have felt good."

Tara smiled at Jim Waller, who ate lunch at Nel's every day and most days came back for pie midafternoon. He was quiet. Never bothered anyone. Always had correct change. But then again, he was a banker. That might be some kind of requirement.

She'd just turned to walk away when Jim surprised her. "Tara," he said, "I was wondering if you'd like to go out with me tomorrow night? There's a nice place in Bluemond that has a dynamite prime rib special on Saturday nights."

Tara kept her smile in place. Upon arriving in Wyattville, she'd realized that young, single women were a rare find in the small, rural town. But she'd politely turned down all offers. First dates led to second dates. Second dates led to relationships. Relationships led to marriage.

Joanna Travis could have gotten married. Tara Thompson couldn't.

Jim had never asked. In fact, Jim had only recently started coming to Nel's. When he and Madeline Fenton had been dating, they'd frequented the competition.

People in the know said it was a stormy relationship, with frequent breakups and makeups, which sounded a whole lot like middle school to Tara. Each episode resembled the other. Madeline would tell Jim it was over, he'd grovel and buy a piece of jewelry and they'd be good to go. Until the next time.

A few months ago it had ended for good. Nobody but Jim was surprised. Supposedly he was devastated.

That's when he'd started coming to Nel's. Maybe to avoid Madeline?

But he hadn't been able to completely avoid her mother or father. On Jim's third visit to Nel's, Alice and Henry were already at the counter. The other customers took notice, of course. Probably were anxious to see if plates were going to be thrown. Tara had seen Henry put his hand on Alice's arm, perhaps to remind her that they were in public.

No words had been exchanged that time or to the best of Tara's knowledge, any time after that. A week later, Alice had mentioned to Tara that Jim Waller wasn't good enough for Madeline. Tara had let it go. If Alice wanted to look at Madeline through rose-colored glasses, it wasn't Tara's job to argue for a good, strong pair of progressive lenses.

Tara was grateful the group had avoided fireworks. She wouldn't do anything to risk losing Alice and Henry's friendship, but she did want to keep Jim Waller's business. Her gross receipts had gone up forty dollars a week between his lunches and afternoon pie.

There'd been another opportunity for a big explosion when Madeline had unexpectedly started enjoying Nel's coffee. It had begun on Monday, following the Saturday dinner at Alice and Henry's. Every day since, the woman had come in, somehow always managing to arrive when Jake was there. Tara was sure that Madeline was watching out her window, just waiting for Jake's squad car to park.

The pattern had been set the first day. Madeline had ignored Jim when she walked past and Jim had shown no reaction. She'd headed straight for Jake and quite frankly, he hadn't appeared to mind.

Right now the two of them were sitting in a corner booth. Jake must have said something terribly funny because Madeline was laughing like some kind of lunatic.

Okay, maybe she was exaggerating a little. And being just a teeny bit bitchy.

It had been almost a week since the fire, since Jake had kissed her silly, since he'd hovered over her bed, as she'd battled back from a nightmare. They'd had a brief conversation at the restaurant that Sunday morning. She'd been pretty shaken by her trip to Minneapolis and didn't recall exactly what she'd said. Had noticed that he was a little off, too, and chalked that up to the circumstances. It was the morning-after conversation following an overnight that had happened but not really. Not the way it might have.

After that, he'd been pretty scarce. Had eaten in the restaurant a few times but hadn't done much more than nod in her direction.

By the looks of things, he'd already totally forgotten about the kiss and what might have come afterward. Perhaps he'd put it in perspective. Heck, maybe he was grateful that they'd been interrupted?

Jake was moving on. She glanced back at Jim. Even he had moved on. She was running a distant third.

"You know, Jim, I'd love to have dinner with you. What time should I be ready?"

JAKE OPENED THE DOOR of his squad car, grateful to finally be away from Madeline. Lori Mae was right. Madeline gave off some strange vibes. She was about as subtle as a flashing neon sign. And no less irritating. But Janet's comments gnawed at him, and he thought that Madeline might offer some insight into her brother. She, however, shut down the conversation every time he tried to turn it in that direction.

He'd done his research on Bill Fenton. He was living in Chicago, working at a fast-food restaurant. Jake thought Alice's explanation of *sales* was stretching it a bit, but mothers were allowed to do that. He'd had no unexplained absences from work and had been there the day after Tara's garage had burned. If he'd started the fire, he'd have had to drive hard that night to be ready for work at five the next morning. It was possible but not probable.

Jake stepped on the accelerator and left Wyattville behind.

He'd already had a busy morning. He'd barely been out of the shower when Lori Mae had called. Someone had trashed the coin-operated laundry. Fortunately, the psychic who lived across the street, who evidently was comfortable predicting the future, didn't like to be surprised by unexpected visitors. She'd had a security camera mounted on her house, pointed at the street. That, along with the physical evidence at the scene, had allowed him to arrest two recent high-school grads who were on the fast track to the county jail.

After he'd wrapped that up, he'd stopped at the

restaurant specifically to make sure that Tara was there and tied up. He didn't want her having free time and getting the idea that she needed to run home for something.

It would be more than a little awkward if she interrupted him when he was searching her house.

The idea had taken seed the night before when he'd stopped at Alice and Henry's. Earlier that day, Henry had left a message with Lori Mae that he was wondering if Jake could help him with the shed on Saturday afternoon. Jake had stopped by to let him know that would work. While he was there, Henry had mentioned that he needed to get to Tara's house to replace some lightbulbs in the stairwell.

Jake had volunteered to do the job. Henry had been happy enough to turn over a key.

He had permission. From the landlord. To enter the house.

So it wasn't illegal. But for most of the night, he'd debated whether it was the *right* thing to do. It was her space. She had an expectation of privacy. But she was evasive and had lied about her trip to Minneapolis. At best, she was hiding something of little consequence, perhaps something embarrassing. At worst, she was hiding something that would get her or someone else hurt. All week long he'd watched her at the restaurant, had practically willed her to tell him what was going on, but she'd shown no more interest in him than she had in Nicholi. Less, in fact.

So now he was desperate enough to do things that he might not normally consider.

At Tara's, he parked behind the house, next to the burned-out shell of the garage. He didn't want his squad car to be visible from the road. Otherwise, Tara would know he'd been there before he ever got back to town. It was okay that there was spotty cell service in Wyattville. People didn't need phones. Gossip floated in the air, and if it was especially juicy, it traveled at warp speed.

He let himself in the back door and started upstairs in the bedroom closet. It was very organized. Blouses and pants on one side, skirts and dresses on the other. On the shelf, she'd neatly stacked shoe boxes on top of larger, flatter boxes. He opened every one of them. She had a sewing kit, a box of assorted greeting cards and three boxes of paperback books.

He opened every dresser drawer and felt his throat get dry when one of them contained little bits and pieces of sexy underwear. He ran his fingers across the silk and lace and thought about how incongruous they were to the long-sleeved shirts that Tara favored.

He looked underneath the bed and in between the mattress and the box springs. All he found was a little dust. He moved into the small bathroom, giving it a quick once-over. He looked in all the cupboards, behind the tall stacks of towels. Nothing looked out of place. That is, until he looked up. A corner of one of the ceiling tiles looked as if it had been pushed up. He'd have never noticed it if he hadn't been looking very carefully.

Standing on the lid of the toilet, he reached up, moved the ceiling tile aside and found a cell phone. He flipped it on. Fully charged. He made a note of the number.

Why the hell did she keep her cell phone hidden above the ceiling of the bathroom? She obviously kept it charged, so it wasn't as if she'd forgotten it was up there. When he went to put it back, he realized there was a bag. He nudged it. It was heavy so he was careful when he lifted it down.

Inside were jeans, a sweatshirt and running shoes. The weight came from a heavy flashlight. He flipped it on. The beam was very bright. It was the last item, however, that set him back. There was a plain white envelope that had at least two thousand dollars in tens and twenties.

What the hell was she doing with that kind of cash in her ceiling? In what almost appeared to be a getaway bag, something she could grab in a hurry and flee. Was it possible that she was involved in something illegal that would require her to run at a moment's notice?

Was he destined to keep reliving the same damn

nightmare? Was he going to keep caring about bad people who would hurt him?

He put everything back, replaced the ceiling tile and moved on to the living room. Next to the old television and DVD player, Tara kept a stack of DVDs. He flipped through them but didn't see anything unusual. Other than the fact that she liked old Jimmy Stewart and Katharine Hepburn movies. There was a stack of newspapers, old editions of the *Bluemond County Press*.

Jake had a bad feeling. It was not so much what he found but what he didn't. Not a single photo album. No stacks of letters or old Christmas cards from friends and loved ones. Everybody had stuff like that. Cops always looked for it. It gave you a sense of who the person was. But it was as though Tara had no past.

Who the hell was Tara Thompson?

Disgusted that he didn't know any more than before he'd started, he left. He didn't put the new lightbulbs in. He'd come back another time to do that.

FOR HER DATE, Tara wore a black dress with dark sheer sleeves. It offered just enough cover for her scars without looking too heavy. It was long enough that she didn't need to bother with pantyhose. She slipped some black sandals on, realizing that she hadn't worn heels in over a year.

Makeup was minimal. Powder, lip gloss and mascara. Even in the evening the thermometer still hovered around seventy-five. Catching a glimpse of herself in the mirror, she thought she looked good. And it was very nice to have something on besides jeans or a cotton skirt.

She was nervous. She'd had a little more than twenty-four hours to think about the date. When Jim Waller had sat down at her counter today, she'd almost cancelled. But she knew that she needed to go. Needed to get on with her life. Otherwise, Michael would have won after all. And it wouldn't hurt to have something to think about besides Jake Vernelli. He was all hot and cold and making her crazy.

She wondered how long he would have to be gone before she stopped thinking about him. It was funny that she'd been able to walk away from her whole life and not spend too much time looking back. But Jake's presence was so commanding, his quiet strength so comforting, his touch so soft, that she thought it might take a long time for the memory to fade.

At six-thirty, she closed and locked her back door. The strap of her sandal slipped off her heel as she walked. When she got to her van, she reached down to fix it. She was concentrating on it when she heard a vehicle pull into her driveway. Her first thought was that Jim had misunderstood the plan to meet, but then she realized she had bigger problems than that.

It was Jake in his truck. His window was down and his hair was windblown. He was eating the last of an apple. He tossed it aside. "What's going on?" he asked. He ran his eyes over her once, starting at her face and ending at her toes. Then he backtracked, taking a long journey upward. She felt very warm and it had nothing to do with the temperature.

"Going somewhere?" he asked. His voice sounded hoarse and she wondered just what he'd been doing.

She shook her head. "Yes. I…I have a date. What are you doing here?"

Jake held up a box of lightbulbs. "Henry asked if I'd replace the ones in your hallway."

"Oh. Well, you'll need to do that some other time. I've really got to be going. Have a nice night," she added, hoping he'd move along.

He shut off his truck and got out. He was wearing faded blue jeans and they were covered with dust. His white T-shirt was streaked with dirt and he had a red bandanna wrapped around his neck that looked as if had been used to mop up sweat.

He got close enough to her that she could feel the heat roll off his body. "Who's the lucky guy?" he asked.

"Jim Waller. He's a vice president at the bank."

Jake considered this. "Tall guy. Thin. Almost

forty. Eats a turkey sandwich and a cup of soup every day of his life."

She'd been right. Jake saw a lot more than he let on. "That's the one."

"He used to date Madeline Fenton."

"A while back," Tara said, dismissing the relationship.

"You can't go," he said suddenly. "You need to call him and tell him that you can't go. You have the flu. You're contagious."

"Jake, were you out in the sun too long today?"

"I was helping Henry for a couple hours this afternoon. But that has nothing to do with it. This is not a good idea, Tara. Somebody has been trying to get your attention. This is not the time to be going out with a strange man."

"He's not a strange man. He eats lunch in my restaurant every day."

"Where are you going?"

"To Bluemond. We're having dinner."

"What time will you be back?"

"What time is my curfew, *Dad?*"

Jake looked as if he might explode. His nose was already sunburned and his face turned red to match. Too bad. Maybe he should call up Madeline and arrange his own date. She yanked open her van door. "I have to go or I'll be late."

"You're driving?" he said, his tone incredulous.

"I'm meeting Jim at Nel's. We're leaving from

there." A date was one thing, a man in her house was another. Not that she owed Jake an explanation. "Excuse me," she said.

He moved fast. One minute he was standing casually and the next, he had her back against the van, his body fully pressed against her. With his thumb and index finger, he gripped her chin. Then he angled his mouth and kissed her.

He pushed his tongue in her mouth, widened the angle of the kiss, and altogether consumed her. It was hot and reckless and when it ended, she wanted to beg for more.

He took a step back.

"Think about *that* on your date."

FOUR MILES INTO THE TRIP, she and Jim had discussed the weather, the shape the county highway was in, and then the weather some more. The flu wasn't sounding so bad.

"How's business?" Tara asked.

"Steady."

She chewed on the corner of her lip but stopped suddenly when she realized that she could taste Jake. It was a combination of the tartness of the apple he'd eaten mixed with the tangy salt of his sweat.

Great. Like she needed a reminder. She was still reeling from his kiss. When she'd driven away, her arms and legs had been shaking and she'd felt as if they might not be connected to the rest of her body. Jim had been waiting in the lot behind the restaurant. If he hadn't been, she might have been tempted to follow Jake's advice. She really wasn't feeling well. She was all torn up inside. Second-guessing everything.

She was no doubt a lousy date. Even if he wasn't a great conversationalist, Jim didn't deserve that. "One of my customers mentioned that he's excited about taking a few day trips with the new senior citizens group," Tara said. "How about you? Been on any great vacations lately?" A long trip could get them from here to salad.

"No. I don't get away much."

"I'm sorry to hear that," Tara replied sincerely. She stared at the passing countryside. This was her punishment for being jealous of Madeline.

Minutes later, bad got worse. She heard the thump-thump of a tire going flat. Jim shrugged and pulled off the side of the two-lane highway. They both got out of the car, staring at the flat rear tire.

"I've never changed a flat before," she volunteered. "But between the two of us, we could probably manage it."

"I don't have a spare."

She opened her purse and pulled out her cell phone. She turned it on and realized pretty quickly that she wasn't getting any service. Her phone almost always got service at her house and at the restaurant. She shook it, tried again and met with the same results. She pointed at Jim's phone on his belt. "Let's hope you have better luck."

He punched the on button. He did it a second time. "Darn. I don't think it's charged."

"That is a problem." Tara walked around the car, wanting to put some distance between her and Jim. Otherwise, she might just throttle him.

"There's a house a mile or so up the road," Jim said. "I'll walk there and get some help."

It was possibly their only option. "I'll come with you."

Jim stared at her high-heeled, open-toed sandals. "Those shoes aren't made for walking. You should probably stay here."

She didn't want to stay by herself. But she certainly didn't want to spend another minute with Jim Waller. He was right about the shoes. She could take them off but it would be impossible to walk barefoot on the hot pavement. She could walk on the shoulder of the road. It would be cooler than the hot asphalt but it was chock-full of rocks, prickly grass and who knew what else. Her feet would be eaten up.

Not sure what to do, she weighed the risks of staying. At least two hours of daylight remained. She could lock the car doors.

"Okay. But hurry. Please."

Jim had just disappeared over the first hill when

an older blue truck pulled up next to Tara. A lone man, about forty, with a Minnesota Twins baseball cap and a gray T-shirt leaned over and yelled out the open window.

"Need some help?"

Tara's windows were rolled up tight but she heard the question. She didn't know him. "I've got a ride coming. He'll be here any minute," she yelled back.

He looked like he didn't understand.

"No, thanks," she yelled again.

He pulled his vehicle directly in front of hers. When she saw him open his door, she knew she was in terrible trouble.

Chapter Eleven

Jake drove around Wyattville for fifteen minutes before he admitted that the woman got to him in a bad way. She'd looked hot in that black dress, and it had nothing to do with the temperature. She'd been all ripe curves and soft skin. And she'd smelled really good, like spring flowers in his mom's garden.

And if the van hadn't been there supporting them when he'd kissed her, he might have fallen down. The woman literally made him weak in the knees. He'd been trying to stay away from her all week, telling himself that she was a liar and there was no room in his life for another liar. But then he'd see her at Nel's, hear her laugh or tease a customer, and his gut would turn. He wanted her. Badly. And he was very jealous of Jim Waller.

Admitting it spurred him into action. The woman was an accident waiting to happen. Trouble followed her around like ants on a sugar trail. She didn't have any sense at all. Going out with a stranger? So what that he ate in the restaurant every day? He could still have murdered women stuffed under his porch. You couldn't tell a thing about people by just looking at them.

He'd learned that time and time again during his eight years on the force. The fresh-faced young accountant took a baseball bat to his wife at night. The gray-haired woman who baked cookies for her grandson during the day sold heroin to his friends at night. He didn't know Waller's story, but the little snide remarks that Madeline had made about Waller still being madly in love with her didn't match up to Waller suddenly asking Tara to dinner. When people did unexpected things, it made Jake nervous.

There was one main road to Bluemond. He didn't know what restaurant they planned to eat at, but there couldn't be many. Tara would never know that he'd followed her. He knew her well enough by now that she'd be mad as heck. But he wasn't worried. He was good at not being seen.

THE MAN APPROACHED HER CAR with a smile and an easy stroll. The T-shirt stretched over a little belly and his blue jeans were faded with a patch on one knee. She calmed down a little. He looked harmless, like she might expect any other middle-aged man wanting to help a woman with car trouble, to look.

"Can I help, miss? I live just up the road."

The irony hit her. He probably lived in the same house that Jim was walking to. She rolled down the window just inches, sucking in a much-needed breath of fresh air. In a matter of minutes, the temperature in the car had to have risen by ten degrees. She didn't want to keep the engine and the air-conditioning running for fear that the car would overheat. She didn't need another problem.

"Thanks for stopping," she said. "I think my friend is walking toward your house to see if he can use the phone."

The man shook his head. "He ain't going to find anybody home. My wife and daughter went to the Mall of America."

He lived nearby. He had a wife and daughter. She started to relax.

"Need some help getting the spare on?" he asked.

"No spare," she said.

He frowned at her. "That's kind of foolish, isn't it?"

Her sentiments exactly. She rolled the window down another couple of inches.

"Where you from?" he asked.

"Wyattville," she said.

"Where you headed?"

"Bluemond."

"Well if you're going to get there, I better go pick your friend up," he said. "We'll swing back for you."

She nodded. “Thank you.”

He took two steps away before turning around. “It’s dang hot out here, miss, and I don’t like the idea of a young woman on the road by herself. I sure wouldn’t want that to be my wife or daughter. Why don’t you ride along with me?”

She might not be so lucky the next time that a man stopped. He could be some loser. “That’s really nice of you,” she said, opening her car door. “I appreciate your help.”

“No problem. Get in.”

He started his truck and slowly pulled out onto the road. “I was hoping that sprinkle we got last night would break the heat, but I don’t think it’s going to.”

It had been the first rain since the night Jake Vernelli had broken into her house. That seemed like an eternity ago but it was really only ten days.

“I know. It was barely enough to give my plants a drink,” she said.

“No doubt you’re thirsty, too. When we get to my house, you can come inside, Tara, and have a glass of cold water.”

“Sounds wonderful,” she said, turning her face toward the window, looking at but not seeing the surrounding landscape.

Tara. He’d called her Tara. She hadn’t told him her name.

IT TOOK JAKE TEN MINUTES to come upon Waller's car. He drove past, slowing down, taking in the scene. The car, resting heavily on its flat tire, looked empty. Cranking the wheel of the old truck, he made a U-turn in the middle of the highway. He parked in the weeds at the edge of the road, directly across from the vehicle.

His gun lay on the seat next to him and he grabbed it before getting out and walking over to the car.

Empty. No sign of struggle. It didn't make him feel much better. Where the hell was Tara?

He looked at the evidence outside the car and was grateful for the sprinkle the previous night. A first-year rookie could follow the tracks. Tara, riding in the passenger seat, had gotten out and walked back to look at the tire. The prints were deeper here, as if she'd stood for few minutes, her dress shoes digging into the dirt. Waller's shoe prints were next to hers.

Had the pair set off for Bluemond, hoping to get picked up by a passing motorist? Had someone stopped to help them? Jake walked fifty feet behind the car. Nothing unusual. He turned, walking fifty feet the other way. There, clear as a bell, on the dusty shoulder of the road, he could see tracks from another vehicle. A truck. He looked closer, trying to see footprints. Yes. No doubt about it.

Tara had walked toward whatever vehicle had been parked here.

Had she gotten in? Had both she and Waller accepted a ride? Jake tried to manage the panic that threatened to overtake him. It might have been someone they knew, someone who recognized Waller's car and stopped to help. They could already be in Bluemond, having a glass of wine, getting way too friendly at the table.

How bizarre was that? He'd gone from being mad that Waller had taken Tara to dinner to hoping like hell that it was exactly where they were.

Jake crossed the road, hopped into his truck and made his second U-turn of the night. He'd keep going toward Bluemond. He couldn't rest until he knew Tara was safe.

TARA DIDN'T THINK the man had realized the slip of his tongue. He was too busy checking his watch and looking in the rearview mirror.

It hadn't been a coincidence that he'd picked her up alongside the road. When he pulled into the driveway of an old farmhouse, she looked around, expecting Michael to jump out of the trees at any moment. But nothing happened. Of course not. Michael was a coward but he wasn't a fool. He'd wait until she got inside, where he'd be safe from prying eyes of anyone who might be passing by. Then he'd kill her. He'd finish what he tried to do fourteen months ago.

Then he'd drive back to D.C., satisfied that he'd won, leaving this guy to dump her body somewhere.

With a flick of his wrist, the man shut off his truck. "I don't see your friend," he said. "Maybe he walked on? Why don't you come inside and have that glass of water? We can call a tow truck for you."

She had absolutely no intention of going in the house. She flashed the man a smile. "Sounds great."

She opened her door, intending to slip off her shoes and make a break for the highway. When he got out and circled around the back of the truck, she changed the plan. She stood up, wobbled and grabbed for her ankle. "Oh, no," she said.

He walked up to her, his eyes flicking from her to the house. "What's wrong?" he asked.

"I twisted my ankle," she said. "These silly, stupid shoes. I never should have worn them." She sat back down on the edge of the seat, one foot propped up on the running boards of the truck. "I don't think I can walk on it."

He looked confused, like a sprained ankle hadn't been a contingency he'd prepared for. "Are you sure?" he asked. "I'll help you."

"It hurts really badly," she said. "Can you just go inside and call the tow truck?"

He shifted from foot to foot. "You need to come inside," he said.

She edged forward on the seat, prepared to bring her leg up and kick him right where it would hurt the most, if he came one step closer.

WHEN JAKE CRESTED THE HILL, he saw her. Saw her, the truck and a man he didn't recognize. The passenger door stood wide open and she sat in the seat, her legs dangling over the side. The man looked up when he heard the truck. He moved, trying to shield Tara from sight. That was all the reassurance Jake needed to know that something was wrong, terribly wrong.

He whipped his truck onto the lane, sending gravel flying. He pulled within ten feet of the other truck. He kept one hand on the wheel and the other hidden, his gun securely in his grasp. "Tara," he called out, never taking his eyes off her or the man. "Is everything okay?"

"I could use a little help."

While her words seemed innocent enough, he knew her well enough to hear the fear in her voice. His gut tightened. The man moved even closer to Tara, his head swiveling from Tara, to Jake, to the house. Jake didn't see a gun but that didn't mean he didn't have one. He could have a knife or some other kind of weapon.

Jake waited for the man to say something, to give

him some clue, but the older man remained silent. Jake shifted in his seat, just enough that he could see the house in his peripheral vision.

"What's going on?" Jake asked.

"We had a flat tire," she said. "This gentleman offered to get me a glass of water."

Right. And Jake was Batman.

More than ever, he appreciated her brains. She wanted both of them to get out of there without trouble. If the man didn't think either Tara or he represented a threat, then it might just work.

"That's right neighborly but since I'm here, I'll take you home."

"Sure," she said. She flashed the man a quick smile. "Thanks for your help," she said.

Jake watched as she slid off the seat. She walked toward his truck, limping.

The bastard had hurt her. Jake lifted his gun.

Tara's eyes stopped him. She stared at him, gave him the slightest shake of her head and kept walking. The man continued to stand next to his truck, watching her every step. When she opened the door and got in, Jake could see the light sheen of perspiration on her forehead. "Drive," she said softly. "Please just get me out of here."

He didn't waste any time. He'd deal with the man later. First, he'd make sure Tara stayed safe. Jake turned the truck around and drove out of the lane, his eyes on the rearview mirror. The man by the truck didn't move.

When they got on the highway, headed back to Wyattville, Jake shifted his focus to Tara. What he saw shook him up. Big tears rolled down her face.

"Oh, sweetheart," he said. He laid his gun in his lap and stuck his arm out across the back of the seat, pulling her toward him. She scooted over, burying her face against his shoulder.

"I need to know one thing," he said, barely able to say the words. "Did he hurt you?" he asked. "In any way?"

"No." Her reply, muffled yet strong, kept him from turning the truck around and killing the man.

"What happened to your leg?"

"Nothing."

"Honey, you limped all the way to my truck."

"I know," she said and then she started to cry in earnest. Big sobs, making her slight body shake. Jake tightened his hold around her. He wanted to pull off, to rock her in his arms, but he didn't. He'd wait until he got her home, safe inside her house.

By the time he pulled into her driveway, she'd stopped crying. She just lay heavily against his shoulder, like all the life had been drained out of her. "We're home," he said, shifting a little in the seat so that he almost cradled her in his arms. "Are you okay?" he asked. With the tip of his finger, he tilted her chin up and looked at her face. Her small brown freckles looked stark against the paleness of her skin. Her eyes and nose were red, and tear streaks stained her cheeks. Wisps of her strawberry-blond hair, wet with tears, clung to her face.

He took his free hand and tucked her hair behind her ears. With the pad of his thumb, he traced the tear streaks.

She sighed, her sweet pink lips parting just slightly.

He bent down.

She lifted her chin just enough.

He kissed her. And when she wrapped both arms around his neck, pulling him closer, pushing her breasts up against his chest, he thought he might never stop kissing her.

She tasted salty and hot, and he wanted her with a fierceness that he couldn't describe or control. But for her sake, he needed to.

"Tara," he said, pulling away from her. "I don't want to stop but we have to. I need to know what happened tonight."

She stilled, her eyes open wide. She ran her tongue over her incredible bottom lip, the lip still wet from his kisses, and he almost caved. God, he wanted her. But her safety came first.

She shifted in her seat and her dress rode up, showing another few inches of silky, soft skin. He swallowed hard.

"We had car trouble. A flat tire," she said, her

voice very soft. "Unfortunately, he didn't have a spare tire. We were going to call a tow truck, but my cell didn't work and his phone wasn't charged. He offered to walk toward a farmhouse to get help. Shortly after he left, the man you saw stopped and offered me a ride. He said he lived up the road with his wife and daughter."

"What happened when you got to his house?"

"When I didn't see Jim, I got a weird feeling. I just knew I didn't want to go inside the house with him. So I pretended I'd turned my ankle. That's when you drove up."

It sounded right. But not exactly right. He'd seen the panic in her eyes and heard the fear in her voice. She'd been scared to death of the man.

"He didn't do or say anything else?"

"No."

"He didn't threaten you?"

"No. Look, I probably overreacted, and I'm sorry if I scared you."

Yeah, he'd been scared. Now he was getting angry. "What's going on here, Tara?"

"Exactly what I said. I got into a strange man's truck and when it looked like it was going to turn out bad, I got scared. He might be a nice guy who lives with his family and right now he thinks I'm a nut."

Right. She didn't believe that any more than he

did. “What about Waller? Where does he fit into all this?”

She shrugged. “I’m not sure,” she said, turning to look out her window.

“Tara,” he spoke softly, “I think it’s time you tell me what’s going on. Crazy stuff keeps happening. Tonight, something else. I don’t know what, quite yet, but something. I want to know who is trying to hurt you and I want to know why.”

She bit the inside corner of her lip. “I don’t know what you’re talking about.”

She was lying. But why?

TARA WANTED TO TELL JAKE everything. But it was such a crazy mess. Was it possible that there was a connection between Waller and Michael? She knew Michael’s family was involved in banking back East. Had Michael promised Waller a prestigious job somewhere? Maybe Waller looked forward to kicking the dust of Wyattville off his feet? Maybe she was his ticket out of town?

It was all starting to make sense. The unexpected invitation. Waller’s flat tire but no spare. At the time, she’d been so irritated with Jim and so relieved that the evening might end early, that she hadn’t questioned his lack of preparedness. But this was a man who always stacked his silverware on his plate after he finished eating. He folded his napkin twice, laying it squarely on top. Then he drained his water glass, setting it just above the dirty plate, exactly in the middle.

She'd never seen him without an umbrella on a rainy day. His shoes were always shined. He defined *anal-retentive.* He wasn't the type to drive a car without a spare tire. Certainly not the type to have an uncharged cell phone. This guy didn't even have the guts to order ham or tuna fish. He stuck with turkey. It was safe.

She only really knew one thing for sure. It was the same thing she'd known fourteen months ago. She needed to rely on herself. She wouldn't lose sight of that. It had saved her once. It would save her again.

"I'm tired," she said. "I want to go inside."

JAKE OPENED HIS DOOR and almost kicked the truck when he got out. He hadn't been this frustrated for a very long time, maybe since that day years ago when he'd come home and found his brother wallowing in self-pity and vodka.

He'd bullied his brother with brute strength. That wasn't the solution with Tara.

Maybe she didn't know anything, Jake speculated. Maybe she was just in the wrong place at the wrong time.

Jake had a lot of questions and very few answers. It was time for that to change.

"I'm going to call Andy and have him look for Waller."

Her chin jerked up. "Why?"

"Because the last you know, he was walking along a highway. He hasn't been seen or heard from. I'm the chief of police, Tara. I have a responsibility to find him."

She looked at her watch. "It's only been a little over an hour since Jim and I left Nel's. It's not as if he's been missing for days."

Jake shrugged. He didn't care. Maybe he'd overstated his duty but he wanted to talk to Waller. The sooner the better. "I'm also going to Chase's house to get my stuff."

"What?"

"My stuff. I'm moving in."

She stared at him. "I didn't realize I'd advertised for a roommate. I'll have to call the newspaper and have them check that."

Sarcasm did not become her. And he'd have been even madder if he hadn't heard the underlying fear that had been in her voice since he'd picked her up at the farmhouse.

"I'm going now so that I can be back here before it gets dark."

"I don't want you here."

"Tough. Until I figure out what's going on, I'm your shadow. Like it or not, I'm your best protection. I've got a gun and I know how to use it."

"I don't need your gun. I can take care of myself."

Interesting. She hadn't said he was overreacting or that he was making a mountain out of a molehill. What she'd said was that she could take care of herself.

"I believe you," he said. "You're smart and just stubborn enough that you probably can take care of yourself. But I promised Chase that I'd take care of his town, his friends. I am not going to let something happen that I could have prevented. I won't."

"So you're doing this for Chase?"

"Yes," he said, proving that he was as big a liar as his partner had ever been. But if he told Tara the truth, that it would kill him if anything happened to her, she'd think he was crazy. And she certainly wouldn't feel comfortable having him in her home. "Give me your key. I'll check the house."

She handed it to him, not saying another word. She waited while he unlocked the door and did a quick search inside. When he returned to the living room, she had her back up against the far wall, like a cat scared of a big dog.

It felt as if his breath was trapped in his chest. Maybe he wasn't bullying her with brute strength, but he was bullying her just the same.

It didn't matter. He'd do what it took to keep her safe. "Lock the door after me."

Chapter Twelve

He was back in less than thirty minutes. She'd spent the time trying to figure out what to do next.

When he'd said that she was moving in, her first thought had been *Thank God.* She'd felt compelled to protest, but when he hadn't backed down, she'd given up the fight pretty easily.

It was weak and needy on her part, but the stakes had gotten higher tonight. Ever since the baseball had been thrown through her window and she'd contemplated the possibility that Michael might have found her, she'd been on edge. She'd always been vigilant with her safety, but since then she'd been supervigilant. But there was a price to be paid for that.

She felt most vulnerable at night. When she slept, it was with one ear tuned to hear any unusual noise. As a result, she was tired, almost exhausted. She never felt truly relaxed. Her routine had been disrupted. Heck, she was afraid to take a shower, afraid to be naked and unprotected in her own house. And after tonight, she was more scared than ever. Joanna Travis, aka Tara Thompson, had never been a fool, and it would have been foolish to turn down protection.

He was doing it because he wouldn't let his friend down. That hurt. She could admit that. But it was for the best. There was no future for her and Jake. Never had been.

Jake had a suitcase in one hand and four plastic grocery sacks in the other. On the way to the spare bedroom, he dropped the groceries on the kitchen counter.

When he came back to the kitchen, he double-checked the doors and the windows and started unpacking groceries. What the hell was he doing?

"I don't think either one of us got dinner tonight," he said. "I hope you like pizza."

"Yes," she said, somewhat reluctantly. "I love it."

"Excellent. We agree on something." He didn't smile but at least he didn't sound as angry as before.

"When I'm in Minneapolis," he continued, "I have pizza at least once a week. I'm going through carbohydrate withdrawal here."

She appreciated the fact that he was trying to bring some normalcy to a very unusual night. She could make an effort, too. "Please tell me there are no anchovies on this special pizza."

"No. I'm a pizza purista. None of this new fad stuff like spinach and pineapple and who knows what else. I like sausage, pepperoni, mushrooms, onions and black olives."

"How about tomatoes?"

He rubbed his chin. "I don't know. That would be stepping outside my comfort zone."

"Please?"

"Fine. But don't tell anyone."

When he got the dough rolled out and it covered a large baking sheet, she asked, "Exactly how much pizza are we fixing?"

He shrugged. "I like it cold the next day. How are you feeling?"

"Stop worrying about me," she said, exasperated.

"Okay. Then start chopping."

It took them another thirty minutes to grate the cheese and prepare the other ingredients. Finally, Jake stuck the pizza in the oven and set the timer. Then he pulled out a bottle of red wine from one of the grocery bags.

He uncorked it and poured it into two wine-glasses that he found in the cupboard. He handed her one.

"I didn't expect wine," she admitted, already drawn in by the heady aroma.

"My pizza deserves this. Come on. Now we sit, drink a little vino and listen to the sauce bubble."

He made it sound so innocent.

She sat on one end of the couch, he sat a respectable three feet away, at the other end. She took a sip of wine, then another. "This is very nice," she said. The muscles in her neck felt a little less tight. They could do this. They could have conversation, a little wine, some dinner.

They sat, both lost in their thoughts, until the buzz of the oven timer interrupted them.

He stood up. "Tonight we drink wine, eat pizza until we burst and then sing songs from old Italian movies."

"Do you know any songs from Italian movies?"

He offered her his hand. "That hasn't stopped me in the past."

They had finished their pizza and were cleaning up when they heard the knock on Tara's front door. Jake held up one finger, moved over to the window, lifted the lace curtain just a fraction of an inch and looked outside.

"Waller," he whispered.

She nodded. Jake opened the door.

"Hello. I'm looking for Tara," Waller said.

"She's right here," Jake said. He opened the door wider but didn't step aside. There was no way for Waller to step into the house.

"I was worried about you," Waller said, looking around Jake.

"I got a ride from a nice man. Then Jake happened by so he brought me home."

The words seemed to come easy for her and Jake

wondered how many other lies had rolled off her tongue. But Waller seemed to be buying it.

"That's good," he said. "I figured something like that must have happened. There wasn't anyone home at the first house, so I had to walk farther. A car came along and they let me use their cell phone to call a garage. Then I walked back to the car but you weren't there. I had to wait for the tow truck and once the tire was fixed, I went to Nel's, looking for you. Your van was there but the lights were all off so I came straight here."

Jake considered the story. It could have happened that way. But Tara had said that the man had picked her up just minutes after Waller had crested the first hill. They'd driven off, following him. They should have overtaken him. If not, they should have seen him farther down the road.

If somebody had stopped to offer a cell phone, then that person should be able to verify the story. "Who was it that let you use his cell phone?" Jake asked.

Waller paused. "Some older lady. Not somebody I knew. I guess I didn't get her name."

Of course not.

"All's well that ends well," Tara said.

"I feel terrible about what happened," Waller said. "Maybe we could—"

"Tara, could you show me where your dish soap

is?" Jake interrupted. "We need to get those dishes done."

Waller looked perplexed, like he didn't have much experience handling meddling friends.

"I'll see you at Nel's," Tara said.

"Right. Sure. I'll see you," Waller stammered.

When Waller took a step back, Jake shut the door. Then he walked over to the window and watched Waller get in his car and drive off. Tires all looked okay now.

"I don't like him," Jake said.

Tara nodded.

"What? No argument?"

"The man didn't have a spare tire and his cell phone wasn't charged. What's to like?"

"I suppose he will come in for his turkey sandwich on Monday," Jake said.

"I suppose." Tara pulled the soap from her cupboard. "Why wouldn't he?"

Jake just shook his head and started running water in the sink. He quickly washed up the dishes. Then he sat down in the living room and stared at the dark television. She sat on the couch and looked at her hands.

Waller's appearance had changed the mood. The laughter, the light conversation, all the things that they'd been doing to push it behind them for just a few minutes, was gone.

Finally, unable to take it another minute, Tara stood up. "Good night," she said.

She got to the end of the hallway before he spoke. "Tara, don't lock your door. If I need to get to you quickly, I don't want to have to break it down."

She didn't bother to answer.

Once inside her room, Tara sank down on her bed, staring at the wooden door, the only barrier between her and Jake. She'd put on a good show about Waller, but she knew how hard it would be on Monday when she saw him. She would have to pretend that she believed that it had been a regular flat tire. She would do it. Her life, and maybe Jake's, too, depended on it. Before, she'd had to protect only herself. Now she had to protect Jake, too.

ONCE TARA WAS IN HER ROOM, Jake called and told Andy he could stop looking for Waller. Then he sat in Tara's empty living room and willed the telephone to ring. In addition to putting Andy on Waller's tail earlier, he'd also called the county sheriff and described the man, the license plate on the old truck and the location of the house. Although Tara had dismissed the incident, in his gut he felt that something was very wrong. If the guy in the truck had been innocent, Jake would rather look like a fool for calling it in than feel like an idiot because he didn't. The sheriff had promised to contact him once they knew something.

He'd decided on pizza simply to have something to occupy his mind and hands while he waited to hear something. He wanted to be at the scene, processing the information himself, but he couldn't tear himself away from Tara. Not after he'd seen the tears running down her face and how absolutely terrified she'd been.

The pizza had been good, and looking at Tara across the table was no hardship. When she'd crossed her legs and her black dress had ridden up her thighs, he'd been hungry for more than dough and sauce. When she'd licked the corners of her mouth, he'd almost begged *let me, let me.*

Waller's interruption had almost been a good thing. Afterward, Tara could hardly get to bed fast enough. He could not even contemplate sleep until he heard something. When his cell phone finally did ring, he fumbled in his haste to answer it, almost dropping the phone.

"Vernelli," he said.

"Chief," the county sheriff said, "I have an update. The house was empty. Neighbors say it has been for a couple months. However, it did look as if someone had been inside recently. A few tracks in the dust. Pipes in the kitchen were damp inside, as if somebody had recently run water through them. That kind of thing. My group did dust for prints, although I don't think they picked up much."

"What about the vehicle?"

"Registered to an old woman who lives in St. Paul. She didn't even realize it was missing out of her garage."

Damn it. "I should have brought him in," Jake said.

"For offering the young woman a glass of water? From what you told me, he didn't do anything else against the law. She willingly got in his truck."

"I don't think his intentions were aboveboard. There's no way of knowing what might have happened to her if she'd gone inside that house."

"You're right. We don't know and we don't arrest people for their intentions. We will, however, slam his butt in jail for stealing that truck if we find him. That will at least give us a chance to ask him some questions."

"Thanks for the call. I appreciate it."

EIGHT SHORT HOURS LATER, the alarm blared. Tara shut it off fast and within minutes walked into the living room. She stopped short when she saw Jake, already up, an empty coffee cup sitting at his side.

"How long have you been up?" she asked.

"A while. I couldn't sleep." Not that he needed to offer the additional explanation. He'd already been to the bathroom and looked in the mirror. Dark circles shadowed his eyes and his hair stood on end in several spots. He basically looked like hell.

"Jake," she said, obviously coming to the same

conclusion, "you need to get some sleep. It's Sunday. Go back to bed. I've got a ton of paperwork to do today. Nothing is going to happen with you in the next room."

"I'm okay. Don't worry about me," he said, dismissing the discussion. "I hope you can get your paperwork done in a couple hours, because that's when we need to leave for Minneapolis."

"What? Why are we going to Minneapolis?"

"That's where my parents live. We're going for dinner."

She sat down hard on the sofa. "I am not going to your parents' house. You cannot just show up at someone's house unexpectedly for dinner. It's rude."

"It's not unexpected. We're celebrating my dad's birthday today. My brother is coming, too. I called Mom twenty minutes ago and told her that I was bringing you. She always makes enough food to feed an army, so one more doesn't matter. She sounded excited to meet you."

The last family dinner she'd attended had been an anniversary party for Michael's parents, about a month before she'd run. Michael had gotten drunk, his father had been even drunker, and his mother hadn't said a word to her all night.

Did Jake's mother ever throw plates? Michael's mother had pulled that stunt once. Eggs Benedict had splattered the curtains.

"What did you tell her about me? Who does she think I am?"

"I told her you were a friend. That's all." Of course when his mom heard *a friend,* she was likely to read more into it. That was a given. But he couldn't worry about that right now.

"I think this is getting too complicated," Tara said. She got up, walked to the kitchen and poured herself a cup of coffee. She held up the pot, offering him a refill. He refused. He'd already had a whole pot.

It's complicated because you won't tell me the truth. "We just have to do the best we can with the circumstances we have. I'll be outside for a while. Andy is coming by to borrow Veronica. He's moving into a new apartment today. I'm not sure I trust his old car to make the trip to Minneapolis. Do you mind if we take your van?"

"We'll have to pick it up at Nel's. I guess that's fine." She sounded discouraged.

"You don't get to Minneapolis much?" he asked.

She shrugged. "Hardly ever."

Right. She'd been there exactly one week ago. At the library.

He walked out and let the door slam behind him.

Chapter Thirteen

Tara was ready on time. She wore a lightweight, long-sleeved cotton shirt and tan shorts that stopped a couple inches above her knee. She really had beautiful legs—slim, yet strong with feminine muscle. She'd pulled her hair up, leaving her pretty neck bare. She wore small gold hoops in her ears and a simple gold necklace. She looked delicious.

And innocent. Was she? During the middle of the night it had dawned on him that perhaps he was obtuse. He'd been assuming that she was hiding the truth to protect herself. Maybe she was hiding the truth to protect someone else. Maybe someone that she cared about? Loved, even?

That was why he'd looked like something the cat had dragged in this morning. Because his mind had been working overtime in the dark hours of the night.

"It's a scorcher," he said. "Must be near ninety degrees. My parents have a pool, so you'll want to pack a suit."

She chewed the inside corner of her mouth. "Okay. I'll get a bag."

Ten minutes later they were on their way. They drove Andy's old Malibu to Nel's and switched over to the van. She tossed him the keys and he slid into the driver's seat. "You're going to need to stop for gas," she said.

Jake pulled into Toby Wilson's place. He got out to pump the gas, and Tara went inside to buy water for the trip. When he was almost finished, he saw Alice and Henry drive up. Henry started pumping and Alice went into the store.

He was inside, pulling out his forty dollars, when Alice stopped next to Tara, who was squatting in front of a refrigerated case, pulling bottles of water off the bottom shelf.

"Honey, I hear you and Jim Waller had a spot of trouble last night."

Tara's head jerked up. "Who told you that?"

Alice looked a little startled. "Henry heard it in town."

"We had a flat tire," Tara said. "No big deal."

"Something horrible could have happened to you along that road. You could have been raped or worse."

Tara's face was pale and her eyes bleak. Jake moved across the store quickly. "Morning, Alice. Ready, Tara?"

They were in the car and a mile down the road before Tara spoke. "She didn't mean any harm."

Probably not. Besides, she'd been right. Tara had been lucky. Would she be as lucky the next time?

"Mind if we listen to the game on the radio?" he asked, trying to change the subject. "The Twins are at home."

"That's fine. I'll just enjoy the scenery."

Like it had changed a lot in a week. An hour later, Jake pulled the van into his parents' flower-lined driveway. He put it in Park and turned toward Tara. She looked up and down the quiet residential street.

"Nice," she said. "Beautiful trees."

"Yeah." He'd managed to calm down during the drive. If he tried real hard, he thought he'd be able to make it through the day. "We've lived here since I started middle school. Chase Montgomery lived across the street."

"Must have been fun to have a pool."

"They didn't put the pool in until a few years ago. I asked them why they waited and my mom said she hadn't wanted to be the neighborhood entertainment center."

"Sounds smart."

"Yeah. I think she was afraid that my brother and I might drown each other."

"That wouldn't happen to be your brother, would it?" Tara pointed to the man walking around the corner of the house, one hand covered by an oven mitt, the other holding a plate.

Jake nodded and opened his door. “That’s Sam.”

Tara got out, too. His brother stood five feet from the vehicle. He had on a white Bruce Springsteen T-shirt, loose blue shorts and deck shoes.

Jake craned his neck to see the plate. “I thought we were having steaks?”

“We are. These are the appetizers.” He held out the plate of grilled shrimp and Jake took two. He handed one to Tara.

“What happened to Veronica?” Sam asked, frowning at the van.

“Hello to you, too,” Jake said. He gave his brother a rough hug. “It’s Tara’s.”

“Scared me for a minute. Veronica’s like one of the family,” Sam said. “Welcome. You must be Tara.” He extended his oven mitt and Tara shook it.

“I just have to ask,” she said. “Why do you both call Jake’s truck Veronica?”

Jake rubbed his chin, looking unsure.

“Tell her,” Sam urged.

“It’s no big deal. A couple years ago, my mother got nervous that I didn’t have a steady girlfriend. She was worried about never having any grandchildren. She didn’t say much to me, but she did bug Sam about it.”

“That’s an understatement,” Sam added.

"Anyway, Sam decided he couldn't take it anymore."

"Secret Ops guys wouldn't have been able to take it anymore," Sam defended himself.

"So every time my mom said something, he'd tell her not to worry, that I had taken Veronica to the movies, or that Veronica and I had gone out to dinner."

She couldn't help it. The story made her smile. And she thought five years had washed off Jake's face. "Your poor mother. Does she still think Veronica's real?"

"Yeah. But she thinks I'm better off without her. She was insisting on meeting Veronica, so Sam got the bright idea to tell her that Veronica stepped out on me."

Sam held up his hands. "Hey, it was true. She let me take her to the car wash. Didn't even put up a struggle."

"Oh, good grief. Your poor mother," Tara said.

"She is a saint," Jake said. He turned back to Sam. "I'm glad you made it. When I talked to Mom earlier in the week, she wasn't so sure."

"Managed to collar the bastard…sorry, Tara, the suspect I've been chasing for two weeks. Caught him with his pants down. Literally."

"Sounds fascinating," Tara prompted. She'd always loved the details behind the story. That's what had led her from writing soft news for the Lifestyles section to hard news, where the stories were complex and often had to be pieced together one nitty-gritty fact at a time over a period of weeks or even months.

"Oh, yeah, fascinating. This guy owns a little bar and grill. He was *involved* with one of his waitresses. Right between the three-compartment sink and the bread slicer."

Tara clapped her hands. "No way?"

"Hey, she likes cop stories." Sam smiled at his brother. "Where'd you find her?"

"I broke into her house. That's her version, anyway."

Sam raised an eyebrow at Tara.

"He did," Tara confirmed.

"He never did have much technique."

Jake shot a hand out and pushed his brother. "I'll show you technique. You and me. On the court. Ten minutes."

"Court?"

"Basketball." Both men spoke at the same time, like they were surprised she hadn't gotten it.

She nodded. "That's how you settle things in your family?"

"Of course," Jake said.

"Well, yeah," Sam echoed.

"Come on, Tara." Sam put his arm around her shoulder. "You can sit on the sidelines with Mom. Dad usually has to referee."

Twenty minutes later, Tara realized that life wasn't all bad when you could sit in the backyard, soaking up the warm sun, sipping a cold margarita, watching two sweaty hunks run up and down a basketball court. Both men had stripped down to shorts and sneakers. The sweat glistened off their bare chests, accenting their muscles, their strength. She watched Jake make a layup, his strong body literally flying in the air. She took a sip of her drink. Lord, her mouth felt dry.

After being introduced to Tara, Jake's dad had joined his sons on the court as referee. Tom Vernelli had run up and down a few times before gracefully giving up. Now he wandered around the yard, peering at his plants. He walked back toward Tara and his wife. "Sheryl, let me see your camera. My roses are blooming."

Sheryl Vernelli pushed a plate of crab dip and crackers toward Tara and pulled a small digital camera out of her shirt pocket. "Take some pictures of your cake, too. That's why I brought the camera outside."

Tom dutifully stepped back and took a couple of shots. Then he swung the camera toward them and, to Tara's surprise, clicked off a couple more of her and his wife.

"Jake tells us you own a restaurant," Sheryl said, as she watched her husband almost lie on the ground to get a shot of his roses. "That must keep you very busy."

She sat back in her chair, oblivious to the commotion on the basketball court behind her. This was a woman who'd raised two boys. A little noise and sweat didn't faze her.

"Very busy," Tara said. "I still like it. I have great customers."

"I worked in a bakery when the kids were in high school. I always enjoyed that. It seems like there's something about food that brings out the best in people."

"If that's true, Mom," Jake said, coming up behind his mother and wrapping his arms around her, "then why aren't you cooking?"

She wrinkled her nose. "You smell. Go jump in the pool."

"Nothing like a mother's love to warm the cockles of your heart," Jake said, sounding wounded. He looked at his brother who'd come to stand next to him.

"I always love you both," she said. "Just more when you don't smell. Go swim. We'll eat in an hour."

Jake looked at Tara. "You going to join us, Tara?"

"Oh, sure." She reached for her bag, looked in it and then looked up. "Oh, no. I must have grabbed the wrong thing. I don't have a suit."

"Suits are optional," Sam said, his voice innocent. "For selected guests, anyway."

"Shut up, Sam," Jake warned. He turned toward Tara. "How could you have forgotten your suit? You went back to get it."

"I know. I should have turned on the light. I grabbed what I thought was my suit but I only grabbed the bottoms. I don't have my top."

"Still not seeing the problem," Sam said.

Sheryl frowned at both of her sons before turning to Tara. "We're not formal here. And it's too hot to talk about this for even another minute. Swim in your shirt and swimsuit bottoms. Then when it's time to eat, I'll loan you one of my T-shirts. It will be too big but good enough while your shirt and bra dry."

She wouldn't need the T-shirt. She had an extra bra and long-sleeved shirt in her bag. She'd hoped to avoid the pool altogether, but this was the second-best solution. "Sounds great."

Tara followed their directions to the nearest powder room. She took off her shorts and underwear and put them in a bag. Then she pulled on her swimsuit bottoms. A tag scratched her and she yanked on its plastic string, breaking it. She stuffed it into her bag, as well. She'd bought the suit for her honeymoon. They'd had tickets for Jamaica. She'd never had a reason to wear it before today.

She walked out and past Jake, who sat in a chair

drinking a beer. She went straight into the shallow end of the pool. She didn't turn around and look at him until she'd walked far enough that the water covered her breasts. Her blouse billowed up in the water, but Sheryl had been right, it was a hot day, perfect for the pool. "This is wonderful," she said. "Aren't you getting in?"

He stared at her, his mouth slightly open.

"What's wrong?"

He shook his head and drained his beer. "Nothing. Nothing at all." He took a couple steps toward the deep end and made a clean dive, barely disturbing the water. He surfaced just feet from Tara.

"I thought you said your parents put the pool in a few years ago?" she said. "Looks like you know what you're doing."

"My best friend had a pool. And a twin sister. I used to hang out there and try to impress her."

"Did it work?"

"Oh, yeah. We used to play Chicken. She'd be my partner and my friend and his girlfriend would team up against us."

"Chicken? What's that?"

He drew back in mock surprise. "You've never played Chicken in a pool?"

"If it involves clucking and pecking, I don't do it."

He shook his head. "No. Let me show you." He dove under the water. In one fluid motion, his hands spread her thighs, he shoved his head through the opening, and he stood up, bringing her out of the water with him. She sat on his shoulders.

"This is Chicken," he said. "You try to push the other girl off her guy's shoulders. The last girl sitting is the winner."

She looked around, hoping like heck his parents hadn't decided to come out of the house. When she wobbled, he clamped his hands down on her knees, helping her keep balance.

Oh, my God. She had herself plastered up against his neck. When he ran his hands up and down her calves, she thought it might all be over but the fireworks. "Jake," she said, her voice sounding tinny to her own ears. "I think I better get down."

He didn't say anything for a minute. Then he turned his head and licked the inside of her thigh. "Yeah. You're probably right. I'll put you down." He squatted down, letting her think he was going to gently lower her in the water. Then he suddenly pitched forward, dumping her. She came up sputtering, wiping water out of her eyes.

"Hey," she said.

He looked very serious. When he spoke, his voice was low, almost guttural. "I guess you don't like being duped. Not many of us do."

"What are you talking about?"

He shook his head. "I'm going to do some laps."

"Jake, I don't under—"

"Hey, how's the water?" Sam walked toward the pool, a towel around his shoulders.

"Great." Jake dove under the water and swam away from her.

TARA SLEPT ON THE WAY HOME from his parents' house, or at least Jake thought she did. She'd gotten in the car, closed her eyes and hadn't said a word. After about fifteen minutes, he'd been fairly certain that she'd willed herself to sleep.

Good avoidance techniques. But it wouldn't work. He intended to wake her up, take her inside and grill her until she spit out the truth. Then he wanted to spend about five hours in bed with her.

That was killing him. He wanted that so bad, like an addict wanted his next fix.

His brain was scrambled and he couldn't think straight. At his parents' house, when he'd watched her walk toward the pool, he'd had a sudden vision of what it would be like to have her long legs wrapped around him. Even in her stupid shirt, she'd been sexier than any woman he'd ever seen. But she was hiding something. Something that could hurt her and for all he knew, others. Just like Marcy.

Yet still he wanted her. That's what had pissed him off and made him act stupid. He shouldn't have dunked her. It was immature. Just that quick he'd reverted back to being a sixteen-year-old.

He'd spent the drive home mentally kicking his own butt and vowing to act at least his real age.

He turned into Tara's driveway. "Tara, wake up," he said. "We're home."

She opened her eyes and rolled her head from side to side, working out the kinks. "I don't feel so good," she said.

"What do you mean?"

"I mean…" Tara's eyes flew wide open, she clapped one hand over her mouth, opened the van door with the other, leaned out and vomited.

Jake opened the glove compartment and pulled out the extra napkins that he'd seen Tara stash there. "Here." He shoved them in her hand.

She sat back in the seat and wiped her mouth. Her eyes were closed and she looked very pale. "Sorry about that," she said.

"I'll take you to the hospital," he said.

She smiled, a weak, silly smile. "This is the second time you've tried to convince me I need a doctor. You're going to turn me into a hypochondriac. It's probably just a touch too much sun. I feel really tired and I have a bad headache."

"Can you walk inside?"

"Oh, sure."

She sort of walked inside. He wrapped his arm around her and together they made it. Once inside, she stood perfectly still for a moment then made a mad dash to the bathroom. She came out a minute or so later. "I think I'd better lie down."

He helped her into her bedroom. "Do you want to take your clothes off?" he asked.

"No. Just want to lie down. The room is spinning."

"Okay. Let me pull your covers back." He held on to her with one hand and whipped the covers back with the other. He helped her sit down, then she collapsed back on the pillow and curled into a ball. He watched her for a minute, feeling the pressure ease once he saw her breathing seemed normal.

He walked out of the bedroom and sunk down on the couch. He grabbed the quilt off the edge of the couch, wadded it up and used it as a pillow. He'd intended to spend the night with her. Not like this, but then again, not much was going his way lately.

TARA WOKE UP when her alarm rang. She had just worked up the energy necessary to roll over and shut if off when it stopped. She opened her eyes. Jake stood next to her bed.

"How do you feel?"

"Fine," she lied.

"When did you set the alarm?"

"Yesterday morning. I always reset it in the morning, right after I wake up, even though most days I wake up before it goes off."

She swung her legs over the bed and stood up.

She wobbled back and forth before she sat back down with a thud.

"That's it," Jake said. "Back in bed."

"It's Monday. I have to go to work."

"No. You're sick. You're going to fall over. It would be your luck that you'll pass out next to the stove and catch on fire. You're staying here."

She couldn't do that. "Janet needs my help. Neither one of us has missed a day since I bought Nel's."

"Good for Janet. She's going to get to keep the perfect attendance certificate. You're not going."

"But—"

"I'm worried about leaving you here by yourself. Do you feel well enough that you could drive in with me? Then you could stay at Chase's house. You'd be just two blocks away if you needed anything."

Tara shook her head. He confused the heck out of her. Yesterday, in the pool, they'd been generating enough heat that they could have boiled lobster in that water. At the same time, she could tell he was angry with her.

The man had dunked her.

During dinner he'd been polite, obviously not wanting his parents or Sam to realize that something wasn't quite right. There'd been conversation and laughter and for two hours, she'd relaxed, content to let herself believe that this was the new normal. His parents had warmly hugged her goodbye but Sam, who'd been chatty through most of dinner, had been a little more reserved.

In the car, Jake had been quiet. During the drive, when she'd started feeling ill, she'd closed her eyes and had been grateful that she didn't need to respond to conversation. Then when she'd gotten sick, he'd gone above the call of duty. The man had listened to her vomit, not once but twice, and then had the guts to stand close enough to put her in bed.

Now, he sounded so worried. She couldn't remember the last time someone had worried about her. It felt kind of good. Especially since she was confident that there wasn't anything seriously wrong with her. If she got another couple hours of sleep, she'd be fine. "Jake, I will agree to stay home for a couple extra hours if you'll agree to stop nagging me."

She could tell he wanted to argue, but to his credit he didn't. "Can I get you anything before I go?"

"No. Just make sure you tell Janet that I'll be in long before the noon rush."

When he got to Nel's, he parked in Tara's spot. When his phone rang, it startled him. Then it scared him when he saw his brother's number. Had something happened to their parents?

"Sam?" Jake answered.

"I liked your girlfriend."

Jake let out the breath he was holding. "You called me at five-thirty in the morning to tell me that? And by the way, she's not my girlfriend."

"Oh. So she's available?"

Jake felt the hair on the back of his neck stand up. "I didn't say that."

Sam laughed. "That's what I thought. I saw you when she walked past you to get in the pool. I thought you might fall out of the chair and hit your head on the cement."

Jake sighed. "She's got an incredible body."

"Don't sound so sad about it."

"It's hard to explain, Sam. She's special but we're not—"

"That might be a good thing."

Jake frowned at the phone. "What do you mean? I thought you liked her."

"I did. She's bright, funny, pretty. What's not to like? It's just that she did something kind of strange. Something I didn't expect."

"What?"

"You saw Dad walking around taking pictures of his flowers?"

"Get to the point."

"I saw him take a couple pictures of his cake and then he snapped a couple shots of Mom and Tara. He left the camera on the table when we went inside to eat. After dinner, Tara excused herself."

"Sam," Jake warned. "I think she went to the bathroom. That's allowed."

"That's not what she did. I got up at the same time to grab another beer. I saw her head off toward the bathroom but then she walked outside. She went over to the table and clicked through the pictures. I couldn't see what she was doing, but afterward I checked the camera. The pictures of her weren't there any longer. I think she deleted them."

Jake didn't say anything for a minute. "So she doesn't like having her picture taken. I don't think that's a crime."

"Jake, I saw her face, right after Dad took the shots. Panic city. Well controlled but definitely panic."

He didn't say anything. He couldn't.

"Have you run a check on her?" Sam asked.

"Yeah. No record."

"True. I checked, too. But I've got a friend at the IRS. Guess what?"

"She cheats on her taxes?"

"Not that I know of. She pays them. It's just odd. There were no earnings for Tara Thompson until just about a year ago. It's like she never had a job before."

There could be a thousand reasons for that. Maybe it was a clerical error. Maybe she'd worked for cash. He recalled their conversation that first night. She'd said she'd lived in Florida but had been very evasive about where. Maybe she'd been living in a beach shack selling fake turquoise necklaces to unsuspecting tourists. Maybe she was a Russian spy infiltrating the space program. Hell, maybe she was really an alien and her species planned to take over the earth.

All those explanations made about as much sense as anything else.

"I can't believe you checked on her," Jake said. It was an empty protest. After all, he'd done the same, just hadn't been as thorough.

"You're my brother. I care about you. You never bring women to meet Mom and Dad."

"There's a lot I don't know," Jake admitted. "I don't believe she's a threat to me or to my family."

"Believe or hope?"

Sam always did cut to the quick. "Maybe a little of both," Jake admitted.

"Be careful," Sam said. "I liked her but I love you."

Jake pushed the end button and within minutes Janet pulled into the lot. He opened his car door and waited for her to get out of her car.

"Where's Tara?" she asked.

"Sick. Too much sun yesterday. She's going to come in later. She feels bad about leaving you in the lurch. I thought maybe I could help you open up."

Janet shrugged. "I'll be okay. But if you don't mind, you can start the coffee while I'm getting the grill hot." She unlocked the door and motioned him inside. "Just give Nicholi and Toby an extra cup and tell them that it'll be a few minutes longer for their eggs this morning."

He'd barely gotten the coffee brewing before the phone rang. Jake jumped for it, concerned that it might be Tara. "Hello," he said.

"Hello. May I speak with Joanna Travis?"

Chapter Fourteen

Jake didn't recognize the man's voice. "I think you've got the wrong number."

"I was sure this was her number. Sorry to have bothered you."

"No problem." Jake hung up. He saw Nicholi standing outside the front door. "Ready to roll, Janet?"

"Bring it on," she said.

He walked out, flipped the sign and unlocked the front door. "Morning, Nicholi," he said.

"Morning, son," Nicholi responded. "Where's Tara?"

"She mouthed off to Janet. I arrested her and locked her in the walk-in cooler."

Nicholi gave him a sharp look before a broad smile crossed his lined face. "I like a cop who has a sense of humor. What really happened?"

Jake poured coffee for Nicholi and slid the cup across the counter. "She's sick."

"She's never sick," Nicholi said.

"Never say never. She'll be in later. Just needs to get a little more sleep."

Toby Wilson came in and caught the last part of the conversation. "Maybe she's got the flu. She should get the vaccine," he said. "I haven't had the flu for years."

"She's not going to do that," Nicholi said. "She doesn't handle medical things well."

"How do you know that?" Jake asked.

"Henry Fenton had chest pains about six months ago. Tara drove him to Minneapolis. While they waited in the emergency department, a young man came in with his arm just about crushed from a motorcycle accident. Tara fainted, just fell right out of her chair. Later, when they tried to admit her, Henry said she ran out of the hospital. He couldn't have caught her if he'd tried."

She certainly had reacted strongly both times he'd suggested the possibility of medical care. Suddenly he felt the need to call her, to reassure himself that she was okay. He walked back to the kitchen. He picked up the telephone only to put it back down again. He couldn't call her. She'd be asleep. She needed her sleep.

"You look confused," Janet stated, looking up from her pancake batter.

"I…I'm worried about Tara," he confessed.

"Tara can take care of herself," Janet said. "Don't underestimate her."

"What do you mean?"

"I'd worked for Nel for years. When she closed the restaurant, I didn't intend to keep working. Tara bought it a month later. She came to my house and said she'd pay me a dollar more an hour if I'd come back."

"So that's why you did it?"

Janet shook her head. "Since I got my first job twenty-eight years ago, I've saved half of everything I made. I got a stock portfolio that would make you drool."

Jake laughed, watching as Janet expertly flipped over Toby's eggs on the now-hot grill. "So you didn't want to sit home and count your money?"

"No. Besides, I knew she needed me. She let on she had some restaurant experience. If she did, I don't think she had much. At that first meeting, we talked about ordering from vendors and I could tell she didn't have a clue. Once we opened, I figured she'd be lucky if she could keep it going for a month."

"Why?"

"She seemed too nervous. Jumping every time a door opened or a phone rang. She looked tired all the time, like she didn't sleep well. I know she didn't eat right. She picked at her food."

"I've seen her eat, Janet. She doesn't pick at her food."

"Not now. Everything started to change about

three or four months after she got here. She started to relax."

"Still think she's not going to make it?"

"No. That's why I'm saying not to underestimate her. Business has doubled in the last six months. I'd like to think it's my cooking, but I think it's Tara's presence in the dining room. The customers really like her."

Janet whipped off her apron. "I'll think I'll just take this out to Toby. I need some coffee anyway."

"Good idea. Nicholi's practically falling off his stool, craning his neck to get a glimpse of you."

A deep blush spread across the woman's weathered face. "I don't know what you're talking about," she said.

Jake chuckled. "Of course you don't."

TARA GOT TO THE RESTAURANT a little before eleven. She was relieved to see that Janet had everything under control. The soups were hot and the meat loaf special was in the oven. Tara wasn't sure she could have done as well on her own. It wasn't easy to cover both the dining room and kitchen. Fortunately, when customers realized what was going on, they were helpful. Many were comfortable enough to stick their heads through the service window that separated the kitchen and dining room and yell out their orders, to save time for the person doing double duty.

However, there had clearly been no time for dishes and there were full bus tubs everywhere. Tara worked quickly to get a couple loads started before switching her attention to getting the lunch special into the steam table. They were definitely going to run out of plates and coffee cups if she couldn't start a few more loads.

She was ladling chicken noodle soup into a smaller pan when the back door of the restaurant opened and Donny walked in. "I came to get my job back," he said.

Tara grabbed a paper towel and wiped the sweat off her forehead. She was still not a hundred percent, and the heat was really zapping her strength. "Why did you stand me up the other night? I expected you and you didn't show. That's not very respectful of my time."

"I'm sorry," he said. "I…I haven't been myself. I received divorce papers the day before I walked out of here. I should have told you. I was too proud."

Donny was a man who had lost a great deal. His job, his marriage, his self-respect. She understood loss. And pride. "Grab an apron," she said. "You're going to need to work extra hard to catch up."

Relief flooded his face. "Thank you," he said.

RELIEF WAS NOT THE EMOTION on Jake's face when he came in for lunch and saw Donny come out to grab a bus tub from underneath the counter. Within minutes, Jake was back in the kitchen, pretty much in Tara's face.

"What's he doing here?" he asked.

"I rehired him," she said. "Excuse me, I need to get these tomatoes sliced or my customer's BLT is going to be a BL."

"Do you think that's wise?"

"To serve a BL? Actually, no. It's the T that makes it. Especially this time of year. Very juicy."

He looked as if he wanted to strangle her. "I suppose when Waller comes in, everything will be just fine with him, too?"

"It's not Jim Waller's fault." It was important that Jake believe her. If he didn't, and he treated Waller differently than before, that might be enough to spur Michael into action. *If* Waller and Michael were somehow working together. If, if, if. The *if*s were killing her. But for now, she had to assume that there was some connection between Waller and Michael. To do otherwise might cause her to underestimate the potential for danger, and that could prove deadly. For her, for Jake, for anyone caught in the middle.

At ten minutes after twelve, Waller walked into Nel's just as he'd done every day for a few months. He didn't look any different than any other day. Tara felt the difference, though.

How many times had Michael told her that the secret to success was finding the weakest link?

Was Jim Waller a weak link? Had Michael promised something that Waller just couldn't pass up? Did Michael know something that Waller didn't want others to learn? Was he being blackmailed into helping? The possibilities were endless.

"Jim, how are you?" She tried hard, hoping he could hear caring and warmth in her voice.

"I'm fine, Tara. How are you?"

"Great. I had a restful weekend. It did wonders."

When Jim smiled at her, Tara stiffened, not because she was scared but because Jake looked like he was about to explode. Out of the corner of her eye, she could see him. He watched Waller like a hawk.

She was barely back in the kitchen when Jake once again came back. He yanked on her arm, pulling her into the walk-in cooler. Tara wrapped her arms around her middle, shielding herself from the cold.

"Jake, if you haven't noticed, we have a dining room full of people. Hungry people. And they expect to be fed. And by the way, you don't work here. You can't be in the walk-in. It's a health department violation."

"What did he say to you?" Jake asked.

Tara tried to give him her best you-bore-me look. It wasn't easy to do when she shook, not only from the cold but also from having to be next to Waller. But Jake didn't need to know that. "He said hello."

"Tara."

His tone said it all. He didn't think she was cute. "Oh, for gosh sakes. He asked how I was. I said fine. I asked how he was. He's fine, too. And then he ordered a turkey sandwich and a cup of tomato soup."

"That's it?"

"Well, he wants chips, too."

"You think this is funny, don't you?"

Tara had never felt less like laughing. She didn't know whom she could trust. The good guys had forgotten their white hats.

"Jake," Tara said, "how I handle things is my business. Not yours. Not anyone else's."

Jake stared at her for a full minute before answering. When he did, his voice was so low that she leaned closer to hear him. "Just remember, Tara. Desperate people do desperate things."

Wouldn't he be surprised to find out exactly how much she understood about desperation? She could write the book.

"Jake, I'm cold. And Janet probably thinks we've lost our minds, hiding in the walk-in cooler. Just give me a minute's head start." Tara quickly left the cooler, making a beeline for the dining room, avoiding any possible eye contact with Janet. However, she'd barely got out to the dining room before Jake was once again stopping her.

"You've got a problem," he said.

And I'm looking at it. The words were so close to the edge of Tara's tongue that she literally clamped her teeth together to keep them from spilling out.

"There was a guy sitting at the end of the counter. He had a hot meat loaf sandwich and a glass of milk. He left without paying. I saw him do the same thing yesterday." Jake pulled his wallet out and handed her a twenty. "This should cover it."

"Jake, you do not have to pay for Johnny O'Reilly's lunch."

"I don't want you to be out the money. I'll talk to him. Tell him not to come back unless he intends to pay."

"You're not going to arrest him?"

He looked uncomfortable. "You could press charges. I'd really rather you didn't. I mean, he's an old man. He probably doesn't have the money."

It was at that exact moment that Tara realized that she'd fallen for Jake. He was a tough guy who knew how to use a gun and thwart the bad guys but he also had a good soul, a kind heart.

"Johnny isn't stealing from me."

"I saw him, Tara."

"Johnny worked his whole life as a hired hand on several of the local dairy farms. He milked cows. That is until his arthritis got so bad that he had to retire. But there was no pension. No 401(k). Not even Social Security. He worked for cash. The good news is that he didn't pay taxes on his income. The bad news is that he didn't pay taxes on his income. He never contributed into the system. So now he lives off his small savings. That's it."

"How do you know all that?"

"Janet told me. Of course, it took me three months to get the whole story out of her. She's not exactly a gossip."

"That would require talking," Jake drawled.

Tara laughed, glad that Jake had relaxed. "Once I figured out what was going on, I realized why there were days on end that Mr. O'Reilly would just order milk. Nothing else. He only had so much money to spend for the month, and when he was out he just stopped eating."

"That's horrible," Jake exclaimed, looking appalled. "Surely there are resources, even in Wyattville, that can help him."

"There are. But he's a proud man."

"But yet he's letting you help him?"

"Oh, I'm not helping him. We have a deal."

"Tara, the man can barely get around. What kind of help can he be?"

"See those flowers on the tables?" Tara pointed to the small sprig of flowers carefully arranged in the inexpensive glass vases that sat on each of the tables. "That's his work. And he does all my window displays. I have the best holiday decorations of any merchant."

"I don't get it. How did you know that a seventy-year-old farm hand could do that type of work?"

"Watch him. He never sits down that he doesn't pull out his pencil and start drawing on his place mat. And his pencil always has a sharp point, just so. The man is an artist."

FIVE MINUTES LATER Jake sat in his squad car, waiting for the air conditioner to kick in. *The man is an artist.* Jake had seen the old man doodling. It hadn't meant anything to him. But Tara had looked deeper. Who the hell was this woman who could look into a person's soul? And what did she see when she looked into his?

He was pondering that when his radio cracked to life. "Vehicle accident. Corner of Third and Flatbush." Lori Mae was calm but evidently determined when she added, "Chief, did you get that?" she prodded.

"Injuries?" he asked as he flipped on his lights and siren.

"None reported."

When he got to the scene, he saw that it was a one-car accident. A late-model Jeep had smashed into a telephone pole, denting the front end. The driver was still in the car, arms braced on the steering wheel, head bent.

He parked, got out, and was six feet away when he realized it was Madeline Fenton. He crouched next to the vehicle. The impact had either not been severe enough to activate the airbags or they weren't working. "Madeline," he said. "It's Chief Vernelli. Are you okay?"

She turned her head, blinked her green eyes and smiled. "I've had better days, I guess."

He did not see any signs of obvious injuries. No facial lacerations or bruising. She was wearing a seat belt.

"What happened?"

She smiled again. "A cat ran out in front of me. I couldn't hit it, could I?"

He stood up and stepped back from the car. There were no skid marks to indicate an attempt to stop suddenly. Maybe she hadn't been going very fast. He opened the car door. "Let's get you out of there."

She swung her legs to the side and there was a lot of leg—she had on a very short dress. She stood, swayed, and he reached out to steady her. She grabbed his shoulders for support. "I think I might have bumped my head," she said.

"Do you want to seek medical care?" he asked.

She put her hand on his chest. "Oh, that's not necessary. I'm not going to get a ticket or anything, am I?"

He could write a citation. There was always something that a cop could come up with. Failure to stop to avoid an accident. Distracted driving. But what would be the point? "No. I will complete a report, however. You'll probably need that for your insurance company."

"You wouldn't mind giving me a ride home?" she asked. "I don't really feel up to driving right now."

It was a little beyond the call of duty and in truth, Madeline made him uneasy. There was something about her that wasn't quite right. But he'd become friends with the Fentons over the course of the past couple weeks as he'd helped build the shed. They'd be disappointed in him if he didn't offer some basic assistance. He'd drive her home and they could take over.

Her car was far enough off the road that it wouldn't impede traffic. Might produce lots of speculation but the town probably needed something new to talk about. "Okay. Lock your car. I'm sure your dad can bring you back later for it."

She smiled and hung on to his arm as he walked her to the car. He opened the door and as she got in, her dress slid up, leaving not much to the imagination.

And his heart rate didn't so much as speed up. What the hell was wrong with him? She was single, attractive and obviously uninhibited. It could be some rocking sweet sex.

But...but she wasn't Tara.

He glanced at Madeline and was grateful to see that she was leaning her head back and had her eyes closed. The ride took seven minutes. When they arrived, she waited for him to open her car door.

"Feeling okay?" he asked.

"Maybe a little unsteady," she said, holding tight to his arm. Her body was close—close enough that he could feel her breast pressing against his arm. He edged away, she closed the gap, and he started to get a real bad feeling.

She opened the front door and the interior of the house was quiet and dark. She shrugged off her shoes. "Can I get you something to drink?" she asked.

He shook his head. "I need to be going. Where are your parents?" It seemed like a ridiculous question to be asking a grown woman, but he really wanted to see Alice and Henry come around the corner and relieve him of this burden.

"I'm not sure," she said. She sank down on the couch and patted the spot next to her. "Have a seat."

The bad feeling was getting worse. He'd known that she was mean-spirited and a little narcissistic from talking with her, but this was proof that she had a screw loose. Had she really dented her car just so that he'd bring her home?

"I'm leaving," he said.

"But my head..." She put out her lower lip, like a pouting child.

"Is fine. Look, Madeline. I'm not interested." He could do this in a nice way. "You're a very beautiful woman and some guy would be lucky to have you but I'm not that guy."

Her pout turned into an ugly sneer. "So my mother was right. You're sharing more than a ride with Tara. Sweet, sweet Tara. We love her like a daughter, Tara."

She stood up and strode angrily to the door. Suddenly her balance was just fine. She flung it open. "Let's be clear about this. *I'm* the one kicking you out. *I'm* in charge."

He was on the porch when she added, "You know she's not really..."

She stopped, with what appeared to be a visible effort.

Really what?

It galled him that he wanted to beg this woman who was nuttier than a Christmas fruitcake to finish her sentence. He was so damn hungry to know everything, to have answers. He stood perfectly still. Unwilling to ask. Unwilling to walk away.

"...perfect," Madeline said, almost spitting the word. "Not. Really. Perfect," she repeated before she slammed the door in his face.

AFTER LUNCH, Tara walked over to the bank, as she did most days. Usually she went later in the day to make her afternoon deposit. Today, she went straight to the lobby where they kept their ATM and a pay telephone. The lobby was empty because most of the people in Wyattville still preferred to go to a teller. They could get their check cashed and pass a little time with a friend or a neighbor.

She needed to call Michael's office. Not to talk to him. Just to find out if he was there. That would be enough. She'd have to be careful. He'd have a different secretary. A new one came every few months. This one, like the rest, would be young, probably blonde and eager to please. She'd be absolutely thrilled to be working for one of the partners. She'd be well-groomed, her speech perfect. And she'd know how to screen the calls.

But Tara knew the secret. She'd give her a false name, something nonmemorable. And then tell the young woman that she was interested in having Michael champion a local charity. It wouldn't matter which one. The secretary would know—any call that held the promise of revenue or good publicity would merit meticulous handling. Once Michael answered, she'd hang up. If he wasn't there, then she would know. She would know that what she suspected was true. He was closing in.

Tara dialed the old, still-familiar number. She wrapped her fingers in the telephone cord, waiting for the secretary to answer. On the fifth ring, she got her wish.

"Masterly and Associates," the young voice said.

"Michael Masterly, please." Tara took a breath, hating the shrillness of her voice.

"May I ask who is calling?"

"Certainly. My name is Mary Johnson. I'm calling to see if Mr. Masterly might be interested in being the chairperson for our annual fundraising campaign for the cancer society."

"I see. And when does your campaign kick off?"

The woman's voice had warmed about 180 degrees. She'd obviously read her employee handbook.

"Next month. I was hoping to talk to him this week."

"I'm sorry. Mr. Masterly's out of town. He is calling in for messages."

Out of town. Michael wasn't at the office. Michael, who never went anywhere, was not in the office. "Uh, yes. That would be fine. Actually, I'll just send him some material in the mail. Thank you."

Tara gently returned the receiver to its holder. She looked over her shoulder, half expecting Michael to be behind her, watching her. But the room was empty.

Tara paced around the small lobby, knowing that she couldn't stay there forever. She needed to get back to the restaurant. There was still two hours of business left.

Act normal. It was getting harder and harder by the day.

Michael had found her. She was sure of it. He'd thrown the baseball through her window. And he'd almost hit her with the car. And when she'd come home from the picnic and thought someone was in her house, she hadn't been crazy.

He'd set her garage on fire and then he'd gotten tired of playing with her and taken the most aggressive action of all. He'd found a way to lure her away from her safe places—her restaurant and her home. But he'd needed help. She had no idea who the man in the pickup truck had been. Maybe someone Michael knew. Maybe someone he'd picked up along the way and it had been strictly a fee-for-service agreement. *Pick her up, get her into the house and take the money and run.*

Jim Waller had somehow become a part of it. Why, she had no idea. But there was no other explanation that made sense.

Michael was probably watching her, waiting for her to try to run again. But this time she wasn't running. She'd left her life once, she couldn't do it again. She needed to fight back.

And an hour later, when Jim Waller sat down at the counter and ordered his afternoon pie, Tara fired the first shot.

"Jim, I was wondering if you'd be interested in trying dinner again?" Tara asked.

"I... That would be fine."

"I thought we might do something simple. How about we grill steaks at my place tomorrow night?

I know it's short notice, but I'm hoping you won't be busy."

"I'm not busy," he said quickly. "That would be fine. Can I bring something?"

Well-mannered scum. "A bottle of red wine would be great." Maybe she'd crack it over his head. "I'll see you then."

Chapter Fifteen

That night, Tara flipped pork chops, sticking a fork into one of them, to test for doneness. Dinner would be ready in just a few minutes. She'd offered to cook while Jake showered. It wasn't because she felt obligated to feed her houseguest. No. She needed time alone, time to think.

Tara watched the flames underneath the fry pan, knowing that she was playing with fire. Waller was her link to Michael. And she intended to get some answers. Telling Jake about the dinner would be tricky. She knew he'd be angry, probably think she was a fool. She couldn't tell him the truth. Not yet. Maybe after she had the information from Waller? Then she would let Jake help her.

Jake was finished with his shower and back in the kitchen before she had the bread cut. He took the knife from her, sliced the bread, buttered both sides and wrapped it in aluminum foil to warm it in the oven. Then he poured glasses of wine for both of them.

He had on jeans and a T-shirt. His feet were bare. He looked comfortable—like he'd been living in her house and eating dinner with her every day of his life.

She, on the other hand, was a bundle of nerves. She put the food on serving plates and set them on the table. They sat down, she passed the potatoes, and dropped her bombshell. "I'm sorry for the late notice, but you're going to have to find something to do tomorrow night. I'm having Jim Waller over for dinner."

Jake looked at her and very carefully set down the potato bowl. "What did you say?"

"You heard me. Jim's coming for dinner."

"Are you insane?" he asked, his voice still calm.

"No. But thanks for asking." She stabbed her meat.

Jake tapped his fork on the table. "No."

"Pardon me?" Tara responded.

"You aren't going to be alone with him. Not in your house, not in a car, not on the damn moon. Nowhere."

This was going to be more difficult that she'd thought. "Jake, it's none of your business. You don't have anything to say about it."

"Really?" Jake stood up, sending his chair skidding back. It hit the wall with a crack. He braced his arms on the table and towered over her. "I think you're wrong, Tara."

He looked like he wanted to wring her neck with his bare hands. His face was red and his breathing ragged. He reminded her of, oh, God, of Michael. For the first time, Tara felt afraid of Jake.

She stood up and backed away from him, stopping when her back hit the wall. There was eight feet between them. Could she make it to the door this time? Or would he rip her apart? “Get out of here,” she said. “Get out of here and don’t ever come near me again.”

“Tara?” he growled. “You’re acting weird.”

Michael always made it seem like it was her fault, too. Frantic, Tara glanced around the room, searching for a weapon. She edged toward the steak knife on the table, keeping her back to the wall, her eyes on him.

Jake lunged toward her.

Tara screamed and scrambled for the knife. Jake caught her wrist. She kicked and scratched with her free hand. He pulled her in tight and wrapped his broad arms around her, trapping her against his big body.

It was just like before. He was bigger, stronger. She would die this time. “You bastard,” she cried.

He tightened his grip. She couldn’t breathe. “What?” he asked, his voice raspy in her ear. “What did you just say?”

“I’m sorry,” she sobbed. “I didn’t mean to make you angry. Don’t hurt me.”

He released her and stepped back, both hands in the air. "What the hell is going on here?"

Tara couldn't stop the tears. Fourteen months of pretending that she wasn't scared anymore, fourteen months of thinking that she'd left it all behind, fourteen months of lying to herself. *Oh, God.* Her stomach hurt, her chest ached, and she couldn't get enough air. She gulped for breath, trying to hang on.

"Goddamn it, Tara. You're scaring me."

The room started to go gray. She swayed.

Jake grabbed her, not as tight as before, leaving her arms free. "Tara," he said. "Calm down. You're hyperventilating. Breathe in through your nose. Out your mouth. Come on, honey. To the count of three. Breathe in, two, three. Then out, two, three. You can do this."

She focused on his voice. When her body stopped shaking, he tilted her chin up with one finger. "Better?"

She nodded.

"Here's what we're going to do." He spoke to her like she was a small child. "We're going to walk over to that couch and we're going to have a seat. Can you do that?"

She nodded. Once he got her seated, he took the chair opposite of her. She concentrated on breathing. In. Out. In, two, three. Out, two, three.

"I don't want to upset you but I need you to tell

me what happened here," he said. "I just aged about five years."

"Someone is trying to kill me. Just me. It has nothing to do with you. You're not part of this."

"What?" he barked. He held up his hand. "Sorry. What?" he asked, his voice deliberately softer.

"Michael. Michael Masterly is trying to kill me. Again."

Jake looked around the house as if he expected someone to jump from the shadows. "Who is Michael Masterly?"

"He was my fiancé."

"Oh." Jake swallowed, his throat visibly working. "I thought you'd said that you'd never even been close."

"I lied," she said. He had to know it all.

"What happened?"

"Fourteen months ago he tried to kill me. It started before that, though."

"What started?"

"We got engaged in August and planned to be married in the spring. In September, I was working for the *Washington Post* as a reporter, covering the candidates for the November election. A fundraiser ran long one night and when I got home late, Michael jumped to the conclusion that I was late because I'd been with another man. He...he beat me up. He hurt me pretty bad. I had a cracked rib, a black eye, loose teeth, lots of other bruises."

Tara heard Jake's soft oath but she didn't look up. There was more. It was easier to keep going. "I should have left him. But I didn't. I really believed that he loved me, and he'd never done anything like that before. He begged for my forgiveness and I gave it to him. Everything was fine until a month before the wedding. My friends threw a shower for me. They hired a stripper."

She looked up at Jake and he gave her a small smile. "I know it was stupid," she continued, "but they did it to be funny and he was actually a nice guy. He didn't strip all the way but he got pretty close. Anyway, at one point in the evening, he kissed me. Just an insignificant little kiss. My friend had her camera there and she snapped a picture of it. A week or so later, she sent a copy to me through the mail. She figured I'd get a laugh out of it." Tara stopped, staring at her hands, not sure if she could go on.

"What happened?"

"Michael opened the mail and saw the picture. I got home that night, and practically before I got my coat off, he was tearing into me." She hesitated, then pulled up the sleeve of her T-shirt. "He...he did this."

She heard Jake suck in a breath. He was staring at her arm. His face had lost its color.

"What happened?" he asked. His voice was hushed, like he was afraid to talk too loudly.

"He broke it in three places. I think when he saw the bone sticking out of my arm he came to his senses and stopped. He took me to the hospital and I had surgery."

She waited for him to take a step back, to turn away in disgust. But he didn't. He reached out, cupped her elbow with one hand and used the index finger on his other hand to trace the *X* that marred her. Up and down. Back and forth.

It was the first time anyone had ever touched her arm. She wanted to pull away, to hide. She couldn't. He held her arm gently, yet firmly.

Oh, God, she thought. She'd missed being touched. She could feel the rough tips of his fingers slide across the still-tender skin. A gentle caress. She'd almost managed to relax when he bent his head and kissed her arm.

The heat streaked up past her shoulder, arced across her collarbone and settled like a ball of fire in her chest.

"Oh, Jake," she cried. "Don't. It's horrible."

He lifted his head and shook it. Then he bent forward again and his warm lips kissed her arm again.

Her head felt light and it didn't seem connected to her neck. She might have swayed because he stopped, stood up and pulled her securely into his body.

Bone against bone. Curve against curve.

Need against need.

"Tara, we're all scarred," he whispered into her ear. "With some of us, the scars are visible. Others hide them better. It doesn't matter. It's who we are, what we are."

She closed her eyes and rested her chin on his shoulder. "It doesn't make you sick?"

"Of course not."

He was rubbing her back and it made it hard to think, let alone talk, but she couldn't hold it back a minute longer. "I had pretty arms," she said. "I know that's vain and conceited and you probably think I'm awful. That I should be happy it wasn't worse or that I didn't lose my strength or the use of my hand."

"You still have pretty arms," he said. He placed both his hands on her shoulders and inch by inch, slid them slowly down the length of her arms. "Firm muscle. Soft skin. Feminine. Gorgeous. Just perfect."

She started to cry.

He pulled her even tighter against him and wrapped his strong arms around her. He rocked her back and forth. "I'm so sorry you were hurt," he crooned, patting her hair. "I'm so sorry."

She kept her face buried in his shirt until the tears subsided. He held her a minute more before pulling back, just far enough that he could put a finger under her chin and tilt her face up. He brushed the tears off her cheeks. "You have a beautiful face, too," he said, his tone very serious.

"Freckles aren't so beautiful," she said, embarrassed to be inspected so closely. She must look a sight. Her nose was probably bright pink.

"Yours are." He bent forward and kissed the bridge of her nose. Then he studied her cheek. "You've got a couple freckles here, too."

How nice of him to notice.

He kissed them, his lips just brushing against her skin.

His lips were warm and soft and delightful.

"You've got a tiny one right there, in the corner of your mouth."

"I do?"

He licked the spot with the tip of his tongue.

Oh, my. She gripped his arms.

He took his hands and gently cupped her face. And when he pulled her forward, and her lips met his, everything seemed just right. It was a kiss of young lovers. Tentative. Gentle. Sweet.

He paused, resting his forehead against hers. Then he shifted and she could see his eyes, see his pain. "You...you really thought I would hurt you? Like he did?" he asked.

She heard the despair in his voice and knew that she'd made a terrible mistake.

"I'm sorry. I got scared."

He shook his head, like he couldn't believe it. "I

would never harm you," he said, his voice low. "I would die myself before I let someone else harm you."

Oh, no. She couldn't breathe again. *In, two, three. Out, two, three.* She would not, would absolutely not, pass out on him.

"Jake, I—"

"What happened to him? To Masterly?"

Tara could feel him channeling his hurt to anger. "Nothing. I refused to give the hospital any details. They called the police and I wouldn't talk to them, either. They knew what had happened. I could see it in their eyes. But when I wouldn't tell them, they couldn't do anything."

"Why?" he asked. "Why wouldn't you let them help you?"

"I was a reporter, trained to observe. How was I going to admit that the man I planned to marry in three weeks was a maniac?" Tara pulled away and began to walk in circles around the room. "But I would have done that," she continued, turning to look at Jake, "I would have taken the chance. But he told me that he'd kill me if I told anyone. I believed him. I'd seen the rage in him. I knew that I'd been lucky to get away with multiple compound fractures and assorted bruises."

"Damn him."

Tara gave him a small smile. "I knew that Michael would be arrested, maybe even convicted.

Then the family money would have bought him probation, not jail time. You and I both know that Michael could have gotten to me if he wanted to."

"So what did you do?"

"After I got out of the hospital, I went to a friend's house, someone whom Michael didn't know. The only people who knew the address were the police. But somehow Michael got the address and came to see me. I'm sure he bought someone off. He begged me to come home, made me all kinds of promises. I realized then that he was never going to leave me alone."

She stood in the kitchen and ran her hand along the side of the refrigerator door. After a long pause, she made eye contact again. "That's when I started planning. I was hurt, in no shape to travel. I told him that I wanted to stay with my friend for a few weeks but then I'd come back. Every night he called me. Every night I had to keep telling him the same lies, had to keep telling him that I loved him, that I forgave him."

"He believed you?"

"I think so. Probably because he couldn't imagine that I could live without him. Once I got the clearance from my physician that I was okay to travel, I ran. I had inherited a little money from my parents and my friend who worked in the human resources office at the paper helped me get my hands on my 401(k) money. In the middle of the night, I left town. I've never been back."

"But what about your family? What did you tell them?"

"My parents are both dead. I didn't lie to you about that. They were killed in a car accident just months before I met Michael. I was an only child."

"And you came to Wyattville?"

"Yes. I paid cash for the restaurant and I bought it under a…borrowed name."

"Borrowed?"

"Tara Thompson is a real person. She's about my age and she lives in a home for the mentally impaired. She doesn't talk or hear. I was doing a story about her, and others like her, when I decided to disappear. I had all her information, even her Social Security number."

"What's your real name?" he asked.

"It's…" She hesitated.

"Tara," Jake spoke softly, his mouth a grim line. "I promise you that I've never met Michael Masterly. But if I ever do, I'll rip his arm off. Then, who knows?"

Tara gasped. "I don't need—"

"What's your real name?"

"Joanna Travis."

"Joanna Travis." He repeated the name, then a rather pithy oath.

"You don't like it?" she asked.

"No." He waved away her question. "I have something I need to tell you."

"Go ahead. How bad can it be?"

"I don't know how bad it is. The day you were sick and I opened the restaurant with Janet, I answered a phone call. A man asked to speak to Joanna Travis. I told him he had the wrong number. He apologized and hung up. I didn't think anything more about it."

"It's him," Tara said. "Oh, God. When I saw the engagement picture, I thought it might be over."

"Engagement picture? What are you talking about?"

"Michael got engaged about three months ago. To a woman that I'd met just once or twice when Michael and I were dating. I thought it was possible that he'd moved on. But then, just recently, I'd found out the engagement was cancelled."

"How did you find that out?"

"Every couple of weeks, I go to Minneapolis. I can get internet access there. I can catch up on what my friends are writing for the paper and I can keep tabs on Michael. He makes the society news."

"The library?" Jake smacked himself on the head with the palm of his hand. "You go to the library to use the internet?"

"Yes." She looked confused. "There are all kinds of ways that people can track computer activity. I didn't want there to be any possible way that inquiries about Michael could be traced back to Wyattville."

"You were being extra careful."

She shrugged. "I didn't want to have to keep running."

"Why didn't you work at another newspaper? Why Nel's?"

"I knew that if Michael looked for me, he'd look at another paper. He knew I loved my work. And even if he wasn't successful right away, he'd trace me through tax records. The paper would have reported my wages. I'd have had to use my real name and my Social Security number. It was only a matter of time."

"But he wouldn't think about you being in the restaurant business?"

"No. When I was with Michael, I could barely boil water."

"What about the man who gave you a ride to the farmhouse?"

She licked her lips. "He called me Tara. I never gave him my name. He knew that I was going to be in that car, alongside that road. I believe Michael or someone Michael sent waited inside that house."

She might be right. Someone had been inside the house. "You think Waller knew?"

"It only makes sense. He's been eating at my counter for months but now he asks me for a date? Why now?"

He might just kill the man after all. "The night at my parents' house, you messed with my dad's camera. Why?"

She blushed. "I didn't know anybody saw that. Pictures are very dangerous. One could get posted online and travel the world in seconds. Or printed and stuck on a refrigerator. You'd told me your brother studied journalism in Chicago. I have friends in Chicago. What if he had a copy and by chance, he knows people that I know?"

"You're very smart," he said. "You were controlling everything you could."

"Yes, but I always knew that it might not be enough. That somehow he would find me. I always knew I might need to run again and I was ready."

He knew she'd been ready. "Tara, there are a couple of things you need to know."

She looked at him with trust in her eyes and it made his chest tight. He had betrayed her and he would not blame her if she never forgave him.

"I followed you to the Minneapolis library. I saw you on the computer. I wasn't close enough to see what you were looking at."

She considered this. "So when you came to the restaurant and I told you that I'd been there all morning cleaning vegetables for soup, you knew I was lying to you?"

"Yes."

"I'm sorry," she whispered.

"You don't have to apologize to me. I owe you one. I did something that I'm not very proud of. Shortly after that trip to Minneapolis, I went to your house, when you weren't home, and I searched it."

She opened her mouth, as if to say something, but he plowed on, determined that she needed to know it all. "Henry gave me the key because he wanted me to change some lightbulbs in your stairway. I found your bag above the ceiling tiles. Because I was looking. I knew it was a getaway bag. I just didn't know why. And quite honestly, I thought it might be because you were a bad person. My gut told me different but I couldn't deny the evidence." He stopped and sucked in a much-needed breath.

She studied him for a long minute and then shrugged her delicate shoulders. "You knew I was lying to you. You couldn't have trusted me. Quite honestly, I'd have done the same thing." She smiled and it gave him hope. "After all," she continued, "I'm not sure I'm in a position to judge. I assumed someone's identity, for goodness' sake."

"You had no choice," he said.

"There were choices. I made the best one I could at the time. I think you probably did the same."

He was humbled by her ability to see it from his perspective. "Tara, you're a good person, a really good person."

"I don't know about that. What I was trying to be

was a really prepared person. I thought if Michael came to my house, I would find some way to get into the bathroom. I would have used the cell phone to call the sheriff and then I would have climbed out the bathroom window." She smiled more broadly. "I guess I can spend that money. I'm not running. I'm not letting him win."

"He's a bastard."

"He is. And I'm sorry I didn't tell you before. I know how you feel about lying. I don't expect that you'll understand. But Jake, if you wouldn't mind, could you just hold me? Just for a little while."

He pulled her close and she rested her head on his shoulder. She felt warm and soft, and he desperately wanted to touch her.

"Jake," Tara whispered. "Could you do something for me?"

He'd slay dragons for her. "Absolutely."

"I want you to make love to me."

"What?" Jake heard his voice crack.

"I want you to make love to me. Tonight. All night."

He wanted her desperately. "Tara, I'll be gone in two weeks."

"I know, Jake. It doesn't matter. I still want you." She pressed her hot lips to his neck.

"But..."

She pulled his T-shirt up and put her hands on

his stomach, then moved them higher, her thumbs rubbing across his flat nipples.

"Tara."

One hand leisurely traveled down his sternum and across his ribs. Then lower. She unsnapped his jeans. He grabbed her wrist, gently but firmly. He wanted her with a desperation that bordered on insanity and he wasn't all that sure of his own self-control. "You're sure?"

She nodded.

He pulled her toward the stairs. And on each step, he kissed her. Hot, long, wet kisses. And when they finally made it to her bedroom, they fell on the bed in a heap of arms and legs. He straddled her, one leg on either side of her hips. He lifted her arms, gently pulling them over her head and held them there, her wrists clasped in his one hand. He took his other hand and traced the bones of her face.

"Stunning," he said. "Just stunning." He leaned over her, stopping when his lips hovered just inches away from her mouth. Then he kissed her again. This time gently, lightly. His tongue traced the outline of her lips. She opened her mouth, urging him inside.

"You're so beautiful," he whispered.

She blushed. "Oh, Jake, you don't have to say that," she said. "I'm in a T-shirt, for gosh sakes.

I don't even have any makeup on. I look like I'm twelve and ready for a slumber party."

"Tara, listen to me." He lifted his head, careful to keep his full weight off of her. "You are, beyond the shadow of a doubt, the sexiest and most beautiful woman I have ever known. It doesn't matter what you wear, it's what you are."

Her eyes filled with tears. She pulled her hands from his grasp and this time he let her go. She reached up under his shirt, wrapping her arms around his back muscles, pulling him to her. "I want to do this. I don't want to think about it or talk about it anymore. I just want to do it. I want you to—"

Her plea was interrupted as his mouth found hers. She wiggled and he groaned. She stretched and he stroked. Consistent with the law of nature, each action caused a reaction.

Jake pulled her T-shirt over her head and unsnapped her bra. He stared at her breasts. Pale skin. Rose-colored nipples. Beautiful. He buried his face in the valley between her full breasts. He licked her, small, wet nibbles that turned into long, succulent feasts. She arched in his arms. He rolled her nipples between his forefinger and thumb before bending and skimming his teeth against her. He tasted her, drawing her deep into his mouth, and when he heard her moan, it fed his greed.

She reached for the zipper on his jeans. He shifted, stopping her. “Hang on, sweetheart. We don’t want this over with before it’s barely begun.”

He unzipped her shorts and slipped his fingers inside the waistband. Her skin was warm and her stomach muscles jerked when he touched her.

It made him feel like he could leap tall buildings or swing from trees.

Unable to wait a minute more, he pulled her shorts down. She lay before him, naked with the exception of her pale green panties. She smiled at him, lifted her perfect rear end and slipped them down her legs.

She was beautifully shaped. Her skin was fair with a scattering of freckles that matched the ones on her face.

“I don’t want to be the only one naked,” she said.

It was all the encouragement he needed. He clawed at his own clothing, shedding his shirt and pants. He pulled down his underwear. She watched, quietly.

“I’m naked,” he said, finally.

“I see that,” she said, very seriously.

Then she put out her hand, stopping him. “It’s been a long time,” she said. “And I was never very good at this.”

His heart started beating again. He guided her hand toward him. “I’ve dreamed of touching you. Of you, touching me.”

She was tentative at first. Playful. And he wondered if he could stand it. He closed his eyes while her fingers teased him. It was too much and not enough. It was torment and pleasure. "Oh, Tara," he said, pulling away. "I can't wait much longer, but I need to know that you're ready for me."

He licked her hot skin. Ever so gently he kissed her. He stroked, he teased, he thought he might die if he didn't have her soon.

She twisted, turned, and he held her. She squirmed, he pressed and she strained against his fingers. Her eyes flew open. "Oh, my gosh. Jake. Do something!"

"Oh, Tara," he whispered in her ear. "You are so beautiful." He rolled over on his back, pulling her on top of him. "I'm too heavy for you."

She straddled him, like a goddess, and he guided himself into her. She felt hot and tight and when he lifted his hips and pushed into her, she squeezed him, making him want.

"Are you okay?" he asked. She squirmed and drew him in deeper. "Tara, is everything okay?" He grabbed her hips to still her.

"Yes. This is wonderful," she purred. She pushed his hands away so that she could move freely. Up and down, she moved her hips. Rising and falling, rocking back and forth.

He pressed the pad of his thumb against her. She threw her head back and flew apart around him, her delicate muscles clenching him tight. Again and again.

He put his hands on her hips, pulled her tight, arched and exploded inside her.

Chapter Sixteen

Jake woke up with a smile on his face. He couldn't see it but he was sure it was there. He reached over to pull Tara close only to discover that she was already up. He closed his eyes for just a moment, savoring the memories. And when he opened them, Tara was there. A cup of coffee in each hand.

"Good morning," she said.

"Morning." He patted the bed next to him. "Care to join me at my table?"

"I'd love to, but there's a man in the other room with eggs and bacon at his table."

"I shall have to kill him." Jake grabbed the tie of her robe and pulled it open. She was naked underneath. "Now I'm really going to have to kill him."

"It's time to get up. We have to go to work." Tara handed him his coffee. Jake set it down immediately and reached for her. He kissed her soundly. When she opened her mouth, he pulled back, knowing that they'd never make it to work. "Keep kissing me like that and you're likely to lose your business.

It's hard to make a living if you never unlock the doors."

"I suppose. Do you want the shower first?"

"Yeah."

"Too bad." Tara jumped off the bed, racing for the bathroom. Jake caught her in three steps, whirling her in the air. He picked her up, carried her to the shower and turned the water on. Cold. But it didn't matter. They generated all the heat they needed.

"YOU'RE A BAD INFLUENCE on me," Tara whispered. "I'm always here before Janet." She looked at her watch. The restaurant opened in less than five minutes.

Jake had followed Tara to town. Tara had jumped out of her van, but he remained in his car. He leaned out the window. "Just tell her we were having wild sex in the shower."

"You're horrible," Tara said.

"Give me an hour and I'll prove to you just how bad I can be."

"Behave," Tara insisted, narrowing her eyes when he gave her a broad smile. "And don't come in for at least five minutes. I don't want people getting suspicious."

He held up his index finger, stopping her. "There is one thing you need to be very obvious about. Waller needs to understand that there aren't going to be any steaks grilling at your house tonight or any other night."

"I'll take care of it," she said.

"Good. Because if you don't, I will."

Tara rolled her eyes and walked away. She opened the back door. "Hi, Janet. Sorry I'm late."

Janet nodded and continued frying bacon. Tara threw her purse and jacket in the corner and was grateful when she saw that Janet had already started the coffee. She flipped the Open sign over, unlocked the door and greeted Nicholi, who was waiting outside. "Morning, Nicholi. I hope you haven't been waiting long. I was running a little late."

"No problem. It's a beautiful day."

Yes, it is, thought Tara. The sun, although low on the horizon, was already bright and not a cloud marred the brilliant blue sky. The grass even seemed greener. The world sparkled with color. She'd shared her deepest, darkest secret with Jake. She felt unburdened, as if a great weight had been lifted. She was free.

He hadn't looked at her with condemnation or disgust. He'd understood. And then he'd held her, keeping the fear and the doubts at bay. And in the middle of the night, when they'd finally slept, Tara had awakened, cradled in his arms, and she had felt safe. For the first time in forever, she had felt safe.

Nicholi and Toby were already on their respective stools when Jake arrived. She smiled at him and could feel the heat surge to her face. He nodded and studied the menu, as if he hadn't seen it before.

Oh, good grief. How were they ever going to pretend that everything was the same as it had been yesterday? It was all different.

But if she wasn't careful, it could prove fatal for Jake. While he'd seemed unconvinced last night that Michael was really closing in, Tara was still sure. There was no other explanation. Jake had promised to do some calling this morning and check up on Michael's whereabouts. She'd been nervous about that but Jake had assured her that he had cop friends who had cop friends in Washington, D.C., and they would be discreet. Michael would never know that inquiries came from Wyattville, Minnesota.

She trusted Jake. It felt good to say that.

She got through breakfast easily enough. It was a great relief to have Donny doing the dishes. She didn't feel quite as harried as usual. However, shortly before noon, when Jake sauntered into the dining room and ordered the lunch special, her nerves kicked in. He rested his elbows on the counter, chatting with the man next to him. Tara brought him his soup. "I told you I'd take care of it," she whispered. "I just want to do it carefully." She was sure that Waller was working with Michael, and she didn't want anyone getting suspicious.

When Jim Waller sat down at the counter, Tara

took his order and leaned close, so that no one else could hear. "Jim, I'm sorry for the late notice but something's come up. I'm going to have to cancel our dinner plans for tonight."

"I'm sorry to hear that," Jim said. "Maybe another time?"

"Absolutely." Tara smiled. She walked back to the kitchen, turned Jim's order in, and wasn't the least bit surprised when Jake followed her and motioned to meet him inside the cooler. If Donny had seen them the first time it had occurred, he'd ignored it. Now, evidently feeling more comfortable being back, he decided to take a stand.

"Hey," he said. "You can't go in there."

Jake stared at him. If looks could have killed, Donny would have been dead meat.

"It's okay," Tara said. "Chief Vernelli just needs a word with me in private, and this is really the only private space we have."

They stepped into the cooler and Tara covered her eyes with her hand. "Janet has been nice enough to ignore us. But Donny's another story. He's going to know what we're doing in here. He might tell someone. Maybe one of his friends at the bar. We'll be the talk of town."

"Tough." Jake kissed her. Thoroughly. And she forgot all about Donny.

"What did Waller say?" Jake demanded.

"He said fine."

"What else?"

"He said that maybe we'd do it another time."

"Tara."

She could hear the warning in his voice. She reached her hands up and placed one hand on each side of his face. She pulled him close and kissed him. He resisted for all of five seconds before he pulled her toward him, his hands on her rear. She opened her mouth and let him consume her.

When she could, she took a breath and whispered, "Want some advice?"

He rested his forehead against hers. He was breathing hard. "Sure."

"Eat a big lunch. You're going to need your strength tonight."

"I'M JUST ABOUT TO TAKE OFF, but can I talk to you for a few minutes?" Janet asked. She had her purse on her shoulders. She looked very serious.

Oh, no. Tara hoped for a hole in the floor that might swallow her up. Janet had figured out what she and Jake had been doing in the cooler, and she wasn't having any part of it. "Sure. I've got time."

"I'd like to leave early tomorrow. By noon."

She wasn't quitting. Tara let out the breath she'd been holding. "Is something wrong?" In fourteen months, Janet had never asked to leave early.

"No. I've got something I need to take care of."

"It's no problem. If you need to leave earlier than noon, we can work that out."

"Thanks."

Tara walked upstairs, turned off the light and came back down. Janet stood in the same spot.

"If you don't have any plans for tomorrow night," Janet said, "Nicholi and I are getting married at six o'clock in Washington Park. We'd be pleased if you could join us."

"Married?" Tara repeated, sitting down on the end stool. "Tomorrow? When did you decide this?"

"Two days ago."

Tara laughed and jumped up off the stool. She wrapped her arms around Janet. "I'm thrilled for both of you," she said. When she pulled back, it shook her up a little to see tears in Janet's eyes.

"This is a good thing, right?" Tara asked.

Janet smiled and wiped her eyes with the back of her hand. "I've been a widow for twelve years. I loved Bobby. When he died, I didn't want to love anyone else. For a lot of years, that seemed okay. Then Nicholi came along."

Tara's eyes filled with tears. She tried to blink them away.

"You know his wife died eight years ago," Janet said. "I knew her. She was a fine woman. Very kind. And when I realized that Nicholi cared for me, I pushed him away. It seemed to me that we were asking for too much—that we'd both had wonderful marriages. Why couldn't we be happy with that? Why did we deserve more?"

"What made you change your mind?" Tara asked.

"I don't know. Maybe Nicholi just wore me down. Or maybe I got smarter. The one thing you learn as you get older is that there are no guarantees but maybe there's no limits, either. You just have to reach out and grab life, every chance you get."

She'd reached out and grabbed happiness with Jake, and her body was still humming with the aftershocks. "I'm so proud of both of you. And so happy for you," Tara added.

"Well, Nicholi said I can't be married in my jeans. That's why I have to leave early, because I've got to go shopping for a dress."

Tara laughed. "He's absolutely right. You're going to have to shop fast. How many guests are you inviting?"

"Just our close friends. Maybe about thirty or so. We know it's short notice. And a weekday at that."

"What about a honeymoon?"

"Not until Christmas. His daughter wants us to come to her house for Christmas. She lives in Delaware. She's got two children."

"Oh, my. You're not just getting married. You're becoming a stepmom and a grandma. How do you feel about that?"

"I think I'll do okay," Janet said.

Tara hugged the woman again. “You’ll do great. Would you and Nicholi consider letting me throw a reception party for you? We could do it here, after the wedding.”

“That would be too much work for you. We couldn’t let you do that.”

“Nonsense. First of all, I love both of you. Second, I’d have never made it here without you. I owe you so much. Please let me do this.”

Tears rolled down Janet’s lined cheeks. “I’m an old fool to be crying like this.”

“No, you’re not. You’re in love.”

When Jake came in the back door, he could hear the quiet murmur of Tara’s and Janet’s voices in the dining room. He stopped when he saw the women, their arms around each other, both of them crying.

Michael Masterly. The name popped into his head. He reached for his gun and scanned the rest of the room.

“What’s wrong? What happened?” he asked, moving to Tara’s side.

She shook her head. “Nothing’s wrong.”

“Then why are you both crying?” he asked, still scared.

“Janet’s getting married,” Tara said, grabbing some napkins out of the dispenser on the counter. She handed several to Janet. “These are happy tears.”

Jake's heart started to beat again. "When's the wedding?" he asked.

"Tomorrow."

Jake shook his head. "That Nicholi. He doesn't have much patience."

"I don't think he's in any bigger hurry than I am," Janet said. "We've both wasted enough time."

"We're going to have the reception here," Tara said. "The wedding is at six and we'll be celebrating by seven. I've got to call Johnny O'Reilly. He's going to have to help me with the decorations."

THE NEXT DAY WAS AS CRAZY as Tara had thought it might be. Absolutely refusing to let Janet work on her wedding day, she had called Donny and explained the situation. Then she'd asked if he could handle the dining room while she handled the kitchen.

He'd shown up for work in dark pants, a clean white shirt and a fresh shave. And done beautifully, even managing to slip in a few loads of dishes along the way.

Tara had fried eggs and flipped pancakes and in between, she'd baked a ham for sandwiches and made big bowls of potato salad and baked beans. She'd whipped up a relish tray and cute little cucumber sandwiches.

Shortly before two, Jake had stuck his head in the kitchen, said that Andy was covering for him for a few hours, and made the mistake of asking if she needed help. She sent him to Bluemond to pick up a cake, ice cream and a punch bowl.

When he got back, she'd just locked the front door. She took the cake box from him and peered inside. "They did a beautiful job," she said.

"Yeah. They said they scraped off 'Happy Birthday' and added some wedding bells."

"I don't think either Janet or Nicholi would have cared. I'm surprised that I haven't seen either one of them today. I hope that doesn't mean that Janet couldn't find a dress. We're going to have twenty pounds of potato salad to eat."

"Ugh." He kissed her. "Yum."

She playfully pushed him away. "Did you get the batteries for your camera?"

"Yeah. I saw Alice and Henry at the drugstore. Alice actually told me to pass along my best wishes to Janet."

"I think I'll wait until after the wedding to share that with Janet. No telling how she may react." She opened the cash drawer to count out the receipts for the day. "Did you hear from anyone?" she asked, trying to sound nonchalant. She did not want Jake to realize how nervous she was.

"Yeah, I got a call on my way back to town. I have it from very reliable sources that Masterly has dropped off the face of the earth. Nobody has heard or seen him in over a month. There's been no credit card activity so wherever he's at, they take cash."

She swallowed hard. "Okay."

Jake came up and wrapped his arms around her. "Honey, he's not going to get to you. You have my word. You're not going to be left alone, even for a minute, until we find him."

NICHOLI WORE A NEW BLACK SUIT, and Janet walked down the park steps in a simple long ivory dress. They said their vows in solid, clear voices, standing next to the fountain. The bride carried a small bouquet of red roses, and the groom had a pink carnation in his lapel.

Tara cried through most of the fifteen-minute ceremony. Jake did his part and handed her tissues. When it was over, they walked back to Nel's.

Johnny O'Reilly had really come through. Every table had a pretty blue tablecloth and a spray of fresh, dark-blue-and-white daisies in simple glass vases. The lights had been turned low and at least forty blue, white, silver and gold candles sparkled. Soft music played, courtesy of a borrowed CD player.

"It's beautiful," Jake said. "The man is an artist."

"Thank goodness he could help. It allowed me to concentrate on the food."

"Which looks amazing. Not many could have pulled this off. No wonder these people love you."

Tara felt warm all over. She loved being here with her friends, the new family that she built. She'd come to Wyattville fourteen months ago with nothing. Now, she had everything. Everything that mattered.

"Let's dance," Jake whispered in her ear. "I want to hold you. It's been two hours since I've made love to you."

"You're shameless," Tara said. But not any more shameless than she was. As busy as they'd been today, when she and Jake had left the restaurant earlier to go home and dress for the wedding, they'd managed to find a half hour for loving before they'd rushed back to Washington Park.

"Don't you just adore weddings?" Tara asked, as she slid into his arms.

He'd never really thought about it. He'd certainly gone to his fair share. Most of the guys he'd gone to the academy with had gotten married. He'd even stood up with a couple.

Suddenly he could see himself wearing that ridiculous tuxedo. As long as it was Tara walking down the aisle toward him. Maybe they wouldn't get married quite as fast as Nicholi and Janet, but he didn't intend to wait much more than a month or two.

He pulled her closer. She fit perfectly. When the song ended, he released her reluctantly.

"I'm going to refill the cheese tray," she said. "And mingle a little."

Three more songs had played when there was a shout from outside. Jake immediately looked for Tara. She was near the front of the restaurant, pouring punch. "Stay there," he said. He ran toward the back and heard someone yelling, "Fire, fire."

The Dumpster was fully engulfed and the slight breeze had carried the flames up the steps and onto the second-floor landing. It was spreading toward Nicholi's door. Janet, still in her wedding dress, stood in the parking lot. She was crying. He ran to her.

"Nicholi is in his apartment. He went upstairs to get my wedding gift."

Jake knew he had just minutes, maybe not even that. The whole building might go. He could hear the wail of the fire engine and hoped it would be in time. "I'll get him. Go find Tara and stick to her like glue." When Janet gave him a strange look he said, "Just do it."

He jumped, caught the railing with his hands and pulled himself up. Once his feet were on the ground, he made a mad dash for Nicholi's door. The man opened it and he practically fell into the apartment.

"Janet?" Nicholi asked.

"She's fine. Look, Nicholi. You can't get out. The steps are gone."

"If my bride is down there, I'll go out the window."

Jake wrapped an arm around the man's shoulders. "I was hoping I didn't have to convince you." They ran to the windows that faced the street. It was full of people, many of them wedding guests. Jake scanned the crowd but didn't see Tara or Janet. His gut tightened. When he saw the fire engine barreling down the street, he opened the window and waved wildly.

The crowd moved as the engine, its siren so loud that it could burst an eardrum, stopped just below Nicholi's window. Within minutes they'd extended the ladder and Jake helped Nicholi descend. Then he followed. Once on the ground, Jake started yelling Tara's name and searching for her.

The fire truck raced around to the other side of the building. Jake continued to run through the crowd. On his second pass-through, when he was looking in doorways and alleys, he saw something that made his heart stop.

Janet. She was on the ground but trying to sit up. He ran to her side. "Janet. What happened? Where's Tara?"

"He took her. He hit me and pushed me down and then he grabbed her."

"Who, Janet? Who?"

"She called him Michael."

Chapter Seventeen

Where would he take her? Her place? Jake didn't think so, but he wasn't leaving anything to chance. He ran to find Andy. He explained the situation and sent him to Tara's.

He took one quick look at the restaurant. The fire was under control. Nel's would have water and smoke damage, but it was still standing. *Oh, God,* he thought, *please let me have the chance to give Tara the good news.*

He was just about to jump in his own car to do something—what, he didn't know—when Donny Miso came running up. The man was sweating like a pig but Jake didn't smell any alcohol.

"I saw who started the fire. It was that woman from the bank. Madeline Fenton. She dumped some gas into it and threw in a match. She's a crazy bitch."

Masterly? Madeline Fenton? How in God's name were they connected?

Jake nodded his thanks and took off toward the

Fentons. There were lights on in the living room. He pounded on the door. Alice opened it.

"I need to see Madeline. Right now."

"It's a bit late—"

"Let him in, Alice," Henry said, coming up behind his wife. He looked as if he'd aged ten years. "We just heard about the fire," he said to Jake. Then he turned to his wife. "We can't keep protecting her. She's going to hurt somebody one of these days. And how will we live with that?"

Alice started to cry. "She's not a bad girl. She's not."

It was all starting to make sense. Bill Fenton hadn't started the fires all those years ago. Madeline had. And her parents had been protecting her ever since. It had cost her brother his best friend, and he'd never forgiven her.

"Where is she?" Jake demanded.

"She's not here," Henry said. "There are apartments above the Double-Pull. Try there. I overheard her on the telephone, talking to somebody about meeting there."

TARA'S FACE HURT. Michael had punched her, dragged her down the street, past the back door of the Double-Pull, then up the stairs to a dingy apartment. He'd shoved her onto the floor and kicked her twice.

But he hadn't killed her yet. She was curled in a

ball, letting him think that she was hurt worse than she was. He was on his cell phone, talking loud, waving his hands.

"Don't come yet, darling. You'll get your money," he said. "You did good. You and Waller can split the fifty grand any way you want. Although I was hoping the whole damn building would burn."

Tara lifted her head just slightly. Michael had his back to her. She'd never fought back before. The bastard wouldn't expect it this time, either. He also wouldn't expect that she had an empty beer bottle up her sleeve. She'd seen it on the ground outside the bar, stumbled on purpose and managed to snag it before he'd yanked her up by the hair.

"You little bitch," Michael said. She heard his footsteps cross the room and knew that he was standing over her. "You thought you could leave me. Make a fool out of me." He kicked her in the back again.

She could not keep her moan silent. He laughed, knowing that she was in pain.

"What was I supposed to tell our friends?" he asked. "My family? You didn't think of that, did you? You do not make a fool out of Michael Masterly and get away with it. You thought you were so smart, leaving in the middle of the night. Do you know how much work you caused me?" He kicked her again, catching a rib.

"I'm a busy man, Joanna. But I'm smart, too.

I know people who know things. You know who knows a lot? The people who work on the computers. It didn't even cost me much. A few hundred dollars and I had your hard drive and every story you'd ever worked on. Then it was just a matter of tracking down the leads. You're not the only person who knows how to do that."

She heard him walk across the room and heard the sound of liquid splashing in a glass. She could smell the expensive rum that he favored. "It took me a while but I found the real Tara Thompson and then when things didn't match up, I found you. You should never have paid income taxes, Joanna. That was stupid. Your address was right there."

He grabbed the back of her collar and jerked her head back. She could smell the alcohol on his breath. He laughed at her. "I've been watching you for a long time, even before that cop bastard that you're sleeping with came to town."

She looked in his eyes. His pupils were dilated. He pushed her head away and it hit the floor hard. He paced to the other side of the room.

"I'm the cat and you're the mouse. You've been scurrying around, not realizing that you were about to be eaten. Weeks and weeks in this crappy little town. I'd have lost my mind if it wasn't for Madeline."

Madeline?

"She hates you, you know that? And she loves

money. So it was the perfect match. And it was just by luck that I found her." He laughed, his voice higher, more shrill than normal. "I was searching her parents' house, looking for the key to your house, and I found her journal. She doesn't like it that her parents love you best, Joanna. She doesn't like that at all."

She heard his cell phone ring but he continued talking, pacing back and forth.

"That's probably her again. She can be a little demanding. And a little careless. That morning, when you were jogging, she could have killed you when she ran you off the road. I was angry about that. I'm the cat. You're the mouse. I wasn't done playing. And the fire in your garage? All her idea. That's when I knew that I couldn't wait much longer. She was helpful, but I knew I wouldn't be able to control her much longer. Especially once she got it in her head that she was going to take Vernelli away from you."

He crossed the room and knelt next to her. He smelled, as if he hadn't showered for days. He yanked on her shoulder, flipping her to her back. She kept her arm tucked close, hiding the beer bottle.

Now he paced in circles around her. "Waller was an unexpected complication. Idiot followed Madeline here, overheard us talking. Said that he was going to the police. But Madeline was a fast thinker. Told him that she loved him and asked for his help—said the fifty thousand would allow them to run away together, to start fresh. That man would do anything for her."

Michael kicked her in the ribs. "I want you to love me like that, Joanna. Do you understand?"

She didn't answer. He swung his leg back to kick her again.

"Yes," she whispered.

He smiled. "Cats and mice can be together. As long as the mice know the cats are in charge." His phone rang again. He pulled it out of his pocket, looked at it and tossed it across the room.

"It was Waller's idea to get you away from Wyattville. That was his uncle who picked you up, but the man was as dumb as Waller. Couldn't even figure out a way to get you to come inside. Then your boyfriend pulled up. I should have killed him that night. He's unfinished business. But not for long. You can't take a mouse away from a cat without the cat getting very angry."

From the street, there was the sound of a car door slamming. His face contorted in rage. "That better not be Madeline," he said. "I told her to wait."

It was now or never. She wouldn't be able to fight both of them.

In one smooth movement, she rolled, pulled the beer bottle from her sleeve, cracked it on the edge of the radiator and sprang to her feet. She held the jagged edges of the bottle in front of her. "Don't come near me," she said.

He feigned surprise. "Well, well. Aren't you full of surprises?"

Yes, she was. She'd surprised herself over the past fourteen months. She'd fought back. Had reclaimed her life. And now she had even more to fight for. She had Jake.

"Michael, it's over. I'm going to walk out that door. Don't try to stop me."

She edged backward, never taking her eyes off him. She was a foot away from the door when he charged at her. She swung her arm, her scarred and battered arm, as hard as she could, and stabbed him. The jagged edge of the bottle went into his chest, right between his shoulder and his collarbone. He grunted in pain and staggered backward. His eyes bulged. Blood darkened his white shirt.

"You bitch." He was spewing saliva. "I'm going to rip you apart." He lunged at her at exactly the same time the door flew open. Jake stood there, gun in hand.

His bullet caught Michael square in the middle of his chest. The man fell to the floor.

Jake bent down next to him, felt for a pulse and looked up at Tara. "He's dead." He stood up and opened his arms.

Tara ran to him and he held her tight. "I thought I'd lost you," he said, his lips to her hair.

"Never," she said. She leaned her head back and looked him in the eye. "Is Janet okay?"

"She's fine. Last I saw, Nicholi was holding her hand."

"Oh, thank goodness. Nel's?" she asked, already knowing that it was probably bad news.

"Your baby is just fine. Smoke and water damage, but you'll be able to reopen within a few days."

If he hadn't been holding her she'd have fallen down. Everything she'd worked so hard for hadn't disappeared at the hands of a maniac. "Madeline Fenton and Jim Waller were part of it," she said.

"I know, honey. I'm getting assistance from the county. They're bringing them both in."

It was almost too much to take in. She had always known that Madeline disliked her—but she had been fond enough of Alice and Henry to overlook the snubs and not-so-subtle insults.

Madeline would have been the perfect weak link for Michael. She shivered in Jake's arms, and he tightened his grip. "Don't worry," he murmured. "We'll sort it all out. They'll pay for what they've done."

Tara closed her eyes. "I can't help wondering if there wasn't something that I could have done differently to stop all this."

"There isn't anything you could have done." He gently rocked her back and forth. "Don't beat yourself up about it. Some people do very bad things.

They always have, they always will. The good news is that most people aren't that way at all. They just go about their lives being decent, hardworking people who take care of their families and help out their neighbors."

She tilted her head back and smiled at him. "When did you get so smart?" she teased.

"I don't know how smart I am. All I know is that these last few weeks in Wyattville have made me remember that there are places where people make a difference, where I can make a difference. I needed to know that."

"Well, hopefully someone will want to make a difference by operating a restaurant."

He jerked away from her. "What? You're selling? You're leaving?"

She nodded. "I love you, Jake Vernelli. Very much. And if you're in Minneapolis, then that's where I'm going to be. I can find another job there."

"You love Nel's."

"I love you more."

He laughed. He kissed her. Sweetly. Tenderly. "I've got something to tell you. Earlier today I got a call from Chase Montgomery. He wanted to know if I'd be interested in staying on as police chief. Evidently *my friend* knew that Chief Wilks was thinking about retiring, even before he asked me to take the job temporarily. I guess he knew better than to offer it initially as a permanent position. Somehow he was confident that I'd come to love the place."

She could feel her heart racing in her chest. "Was he right?"

"Yes, although I made him sweat for a couple minutes before I told him that this wide spot in the road has unexpected attractions and I'd be delighted to continue on." He dropped to one knee. "I love you. I will love you forever. Marry me, Tara. Joanna," he corrected, with a smile. "Make me the happiest man in the world."

She reached for his hands, pulled him up and kissed him. "I can't wait to call Johnny O'Reilly and tell him I'm going to need help with another wedding. My own."

* * * * *